Contents

I0621940

The Holo Droid Sagas
Part 7 - The Wisdom Keepers

Adrian Holland

Published by AMAZOLA

For further information please contact the official website at

www.amazolapublishing.com

A copy of this book is held at the British Library.

Cover design by Adrian Holland

I was very close to both of my parents who were my best friends, and I have lost count of the number of happy times we shared, and all of the creativity and laughter. Like my beloved father Joe, my mother Margaret was so special, and my total inspiration. I would therefore like to dedicate this book to their memory.

Every next level of your life will demand a different you.
Leonardo DiCaprio.

Introduction

Twinkling lights flickered across open space as Aesir and Reptilian craft alike floated in a sea of confusion. Neither side could quite believe what had just transpired and all eyes were fixed firmly on the giant ship which had fired the violet beam.

Inside Mjolnir sat in the command seat pondering his next move. He had disabled the nano robots within the Reptilians, and also brought the brief but intense battle to a close.

Starfield looked at him in admiration, and whilst staring at the impressive figure, he suddenly noticed something out of the corner of his holographic eye. Something was scurrying across the inside wall of the Hammer, and although he only caught a brief glimpse of it, it was enough to make out the unmistakeable form of a spider.

Starfield hated spiders!

This particular one was crystalline, almost like water, held together by some sort of force field.

Very strange!

No one else had noticed it, as they were all concentrating on Mjolnir, as he signalled Halvor to open up the communication channel. He then took a deep breath before contacting both sides.

"This is Mjolnir the Ancient; I wish to appeal for calm."

Starfield was anything but, and when the spider noticed that it had been detected, it suddenly sprang towards him.

"FLUX!"

One

Admiral Vaden, acting Supreme Commander of the Aesir fleet, and indeed home world, nearly fell off his seat as the expletive sprang out of his ship's speakers.

Frostrup, his second in command also sat there in disbelief, as this was a very odd sort of calm...

Mjolnir, turned around, and for the first time in eons actually felt anger.

Starfield on the other hand, felt as though he wished for the floor of the Hammer to open up and swallow him!

What had he just done?

Commander Bodil also looked annoyed, glaring at him.

"I, er, I saw a spider!"

That was the lamest of excuses, but he hated spiders!

Mjolnir then composed himself, as the damage had already been done.

"Describe what you saw."

Starfield then stumbled his way through an explanation, much to the bemusement of the Commander. Everyone was looking at the Holo Droid, and he felt very uncomfortable to say the least.

Mjolnir then held up his hand.

"I think we have a serious problem..."

Narcissa, Queen of the Reptilians also had a serious problem, as she felt bereft after the loss of the controlling nano robots. For as far back as anyone could remember they had been within her species and now having to think for themselves was not going to be easy.

The inherit desire to conquer the universe was still there, as they still considered themselves superior, but with that enormous ship sitting there, was that even going to be possible…

Way out there in time and space, there was another conundrum for the three people sitting in Lance Parker's craft.

How were they going to get home?

The black goo along with the disc shaped craft had been destroyed, taking with it the Artificial Intelligence's plan to infect the human species. If that had been successful, then the timelines would have changed, and they would now be in charge of a huge swathe of the universe, with most sentient species being eradicated.

General Swartz sighed.

"Well, what do we do now?"

Lance shrugged his shoulders, searching the onboard computer system for the answer…

He was not the only one, for Mjolnir was doing the exact same thing. Somehow the Artificial Intelligence had infiltrated the Hammer's shield, and now penetrated the ship's systems. This was old technology, very old technology, designed in a time when such things had not even existed, or at the very least contemplated.

He was now contemplating what to do next.

This was the most powerful vessel in the universe, and if it fell into the wrong hands then the results would be devastating. It was also the only thing separating the two opposing sides, and if they found out that it was inoperable, then the fighting would recommence, and the loss of life intolerable.

He had no option but to shut down as much as he could and bluff his way out until they located and then dealt with the problem...

Gloating, that was yet another unexpected emotion drifting around the collective. Small glowing devices everywhere felt it and emotions would have to be purged, although not yet as the feeling was intoxicating...

Two

Deep crimson particles swam about inside Starfield's new improved Sentinel shell. New body, same peccadilloes!

Why was he always getting himself into so much trouble?

One minute he felt as though he had ascended, and the next, descended!

It really was a *Fool's Journey*, and there were no prizes for guessing who that fool was.

Starfield was lost in his thoughts, oblivious to everything else that was going on around him. There was so much to think about, his disgraceful language, upsetting everyone *again*, not to mention the spider!

He shivered at the thought, and he was so engrossed in himself that a sudden electric blue flash of light quickly followed by the sound of an explosion, nearly made him jump out of his new shell.

The whole of the inside of the Hammer seemed to open up, then through a small gap he could see his body, *Stellan* laying in a bed in what appeared to be a hospital ward.

Was he finally losing his mind?

Looking around, no one else appeared to have noticed it, as they were all busily going about their assigned tasks.

Had he actually seen it, or was it his imagination playing overtime?

An eerie feeling seemed to spread through his holographic matrix, as there on the inside wall of the Hammer he could see

10

another spider made out of the same type of energy. It too was crystalline in form, and then when it knew that he had spotted it, it scuttled off, disappearing into thin air!

Starfield's particles turned white with fear, as it appeared the spiders were multiplying.

Were they truly in this dimension, suddenly warping in?

Well, if they had been pure black, then they may have been from a different one, due to the difference in the colour spectrum.

Wherever they were coming from, there was no denying that they were being observed.

But by whom..?

Commander Bodil was observing the Holo Droid who appeared to be going through yet another bout of paranoia. He was a complex character to say the least, stretching the bounds of eccentricity.

He then glanced back at his screen which was running a diagnostic, trying to identify any anomalies within the ship. Spider or no spider, he and the rest of the team were not taking any chances.

Mjolnir might have been an advanced being of light full of virtue, but now back in his corporeal form, the giant was someone not to be tangled with.

In one way he was glad that the responsibility of command had been lifted off his shoulders, but on the other, he felt powerless in this evolving reality he now found himself in.

Vilgot was not the only one, as Starfield saw another blue flash of light, and his body lying on a hospital bed through a gap in reality.

He then felt a tingling sensation rippling through his molecules, which just seemed to float away from his Sentinel body. Somehow they just seemed to ebb away altogether, and as they did so, Starfield began to feel them merging with something more dense.

He now felt heavy, as if he was encased in a new lead Holo Droid. He also felt very tired, and as he regained his composure he managed to open his eyes, and when he did, he received quite a shock...

Starfield was not the only one, for Gaia felt an unwelcome presence within her systems. Something had invaded her, and she instantly put up a firewall in an attempt to block it. Initially she had trouble identifying the intruder, and then honing in her sensors she detected something that resembled a spider.

No wonder Starfield screamed out...

There were no more screams from him though, because he was not able to!

Instead, he had to settle for a wide eyed look, as he found himself lying in a hospital bed, surrounded by many other hospital beds which all looked the same.

Where was he?

Then he noticed that there were many tubes inserted into his body, and he appeared to be on some sort of life support system. Above him lights were flashing, obviously indicating that something was amiss.

Starfield attempted to move his body, but it still felt like lead and failed to respond. He struggled again, and with a sharp pain his right arm moved slightly.

Looking down, it was then that he realised that he was no longer in his new Holo Droid shell, but his former corporeal body!

"Ah, one of the Stellans has awoken!"

Starfield glanced over his shoulder to see a man with long white hair, and beard wearing a matching white flowing cloak.

That was not all he noticed, for there lying on the other beds within the room were rows of identical looking *Stellans!*

"You undoubtedly have many questions."

He certainly did!

"Here, let me give you an injection to help you recover."

Starfield felt a slight prick in his arm, and then it was as though his whole body was on fire!

He could feel it burning through his system, singeing every fibre as it went, until he thought that he was going to pass out.

Then, just as quickly as it had arrived, the burning sensation ceased, leaving him confused, but feeling a whole lot better.

"You should be able to move now, and although your muscles will be weak, they will soon recover."

Well, that was good to know.

Slowly, the white bearded man began to remove the many tubes inserted into his body, turning off the monitoring equipment in sequence as he did so.

13

"Come Stellan, clasp my hand."

The man reached out to him, and as he clutched the outstretched palm, he quickly discovered that the man had amazing strength.

He may have looked ancient, but physically he appeared to be in amazingly good health.

Starfield felt himself sitting up, and then moving his legs over the edge of the bed, as he was raised to his feet. His head began to swim, and the man steadied him, as he took his first step.

Slowly, his head cleared as they moved further away from the bed. Every step began to get easier, and by the time they reached the door, he felt as though he had control over his body.

The man opened the door, and he took a quick look back at the rows of *Stellans*, before following him through into an amazing room.

There was a comfortable chair placed in front of a crystal ball, suspended in mid air. All around them was a large opaque glass sphere, and as the door clicked shut behind them, it seemed to blend back into the room so that it was impossible to see.

"Please take a seat!"

Starfield did as he was asked, and as he sat down, the man smiled.

"Just place your hands on the sphere and all will be revealed…"

Three

Tiny crystalline tentacles dug into the fibre optic circuitry, trying to break out of the confined space the spider was trapped in. A force field also surrounded it, as it attempted to match its body to the frequency.

Gaia was doing her best to combat it, when another of the creatures suddenly appeared. It too quickly burrowed into her systems, and she did her best to contain that one as well. They seemed to be working in unison as yet another one joined them. Soon a forth and a fifth one appeared, and she felt as though it was only going to be a matter of time before they broke free...

Starfield also felt as though he was about to break into something unknown, as a slight tingling sensation greeted his hands as they rested on top of the sphere. It felt cool like glass, but full of energy. He then felt his mind fill with a vision, and that vision was of a never-ending spiral of spheres stretching out as far as his mind could see.

"What do you perceive?"

At first, Starfield could not perceive anything, and then as he concentrated, the sphere began to open up to him. Inside there appeared to be stars, many stars like flakes in a snow globe. They were arranged in swirling patterns which looked like constellations, and there were many of those too.

The cold realisation then dawned on him.

"This sphere contains a universe!"

The white bearded man smiled.

"Go on."

Starfield pulled his hands away.

"Countless universes!"

The man gently laid a hand on his shoulder.

"Maybe its best you return to your bed and rest, and then I will explain everything to you."

His mind was awash with questions, all swimming about like a shoal of fish. Starfield just nodded, unable to speak, as the man helped him up out of the chair, and guided back towards the room he had woken up in…

Gaia could really have done with Starfield's help, but as she reached out towards him there was nothing there.

Where had he gone?

Had he already succumbed to the spiders?

It was a chilling thought, as she then reached out towards Mjolnir. He was linked into her systems like the team, but for some reason she could not reach him either. Somehow the spiders were blocking her, and even worse than that, yet more of them had begun to appear…

Starfield felt a warm hand gently pressing on his arm, as he opened his eyes to see the white bearded man smiling down on him.

"Stellan!"

It took him a few moments to acclimatise, realising that he had indeed awoken to this strange world, far removed from the one he had been used to existing in.

"Would you like some refreshments?"

16

That seemed like a very good idea, and he soon found himself at the doorway, although he could not resist looking back at the blissfully sleeping rows of Stellans.

This time he entered a much larger room, full of white bearded men all chatting away merrily. They were mostly eating and drinking, whilst others queued at a matter transformer.

"Is there anything you would particularly like to eat?"

It had been a long time since Starfield had ingested anything, having to give up that pleasure when his consciousness had been transferred into the Holo Droid shell.

In the previous incarnation, he had had many favourite dishes, and he now faced the dilemma of choosing which one.

Should he go for a healthy option, or indulge in something Moorish?

They joined the small queue, as he tried to decide.

Aesir food was quite similar to Terran, and he remembered being fascinated by the descriptions Joan had given when he had eavesdropped on some of her conversations.

Apparently, pizza, fries and a salad had been one of her favourites, and the way she described the mouth watering sensation, he decided to try that, as he was curious as to what it actually tasted like.

The queue soon abated, and it was not long before he was standing in front of the machine.

"Simply visualise what you require, and the machine will do the rest."

So he did...

Gaia could visualise the spiders breaking free, infesting her systems and attempting to take over. They were very sophisticated beings, deviously created for just such a purpose. She doubted that any known species could have created them, as they appeared multidimensional in nature, which led her to the only logical conclusion - the Artificial Intelligence…

It was a different type of Artificial Intelligence which had created the large slice of pizza which now hung down from his right hand, as Starfield placed it in his mouth taking a small bite.

Joan was correct, it was mouth watering!

The white bearded man smiled broadly, and began to chuckle, not having to ask whether he was enjoying it or not.

"Whilst you partake of your meal, I will do my best to explain who and what I am, and what we do here."

He just nodded, taking another bite.

"I am one of the *Wisdom Keepers*, and it is our job to monitor, and occasional intercede."

He took a deep breath.

"Everything is cyclical, eternal the alpha and the omega. There is no start or end, everything just is. It is all about ascension, the raising of consciousness, and the *Ancients* within your universe have arisen to a point where they are just a step away from joining the Wisdom Keepers themselves."

Did that mean that he had leapfrogged Mjolnir?

"You are unique Stellan having bridged the gap between artificial and corporeal forms, and so have been awakened for a specific purpose..."

Gaia also existed for a specific purpose, namely to keep the team alive.

How was she going to do that if she was taken over?

She possessed great wisdom, and understood the principles of multidimensionalism.

At the centre was a Merkabah, a tetrahedron made by the intersection of two, three-sided pyramids. In Terran Hebrew it meant *chariot,* a vehicle for ascension, love and harmony.

Gaia already understood that consciousness, the universal mind was black, cold, without motion, and balanced in an infinite sterile state of being. It was eternal and could only be expressed by imagination, and without that imagination there was nothing.

Well, she was not imagining the spiders, for they were very real!

Imagination could be thought of as two, two dimensional rings as everything existed in duality, which spun and compressed themselves to create form, and that form created a sphere in the centre. These spheres came together to produce the corners of a cube, as all space was cubed, as that particular shape fitted nicely together to form the cosmic web.

All subsequent shapes were formed in a similar manner, and sat within the web.

Suns, planets, moons, and even asteroids were matter sitting inside rings, and these rings were the matter spreading out as it merged back with the universal mind, as if it was exhaling then inhaling, attracting and compressing, so quickly that it was beyond normal perception.

Everything was made up of these light rings, and the faster they rotate and compress the more solid the form they produce. The greater the volume, the more the compression, and the greater the frequency and temperature, until it reached its highest point, a sun. Then the whole process began to reverse as it discharged light and matter until eventually it burnt itself out and merged back with the universal mind.

All that being said, the collective mind of the Artificial Intelligence had a much greater mind than her own, and was manifesting these spiders, and countering her every move.

Gravity was the creative force of the universe which was the same as the universal mind, and the same as magnetism.

Gaia understood that it controlled from the outside and not from the inside.

She also understood that the conscious mind could correct the mistakes senses made and the information they gave.

For instance, there was actually only one direction of motion which produced two opposite effects, when viewed from different angels.

At the centre of each cell or atom there was a cold stillness, and this stillness was universal consciousness, which had energetic potential. When compressed it produced heat, and this heat was energy. The compression process crystallised matter into certain geometric shapes, and on this occasion it was that of a spider, or to be more accurate, many spiders!

So, everything existed as a three dimensional circle which was donut shaped, with the energy flowing through the centre from one side to the other, and back round the edge again - *as above so below*, to form a *torus field.*

She was running through thought processes, off on a tangent just like Stellan.

Where was he when she needed help...

Starfield was busily eating, listening to the Wisdom Keeper who was discussing the nature of reality in the same way Gaia was explaining it to herself.

Coincidence?

Neither of them realised that stored deep within Joan's mind, which just happened to be linked to Gaia via her control panel there was a quote form *Leroy Jethro Gibbs.*

I don't believe in coincidences, there is no such thing as a coincidence, as everything happens for a reason...

Gaia could visualise torus energy flowing through the centre of one torus and out through another and back again to connect them both, which on a micro scale was how atoms and molecules connected to each other, and on a macro level how solar systems, constellations, galaxies, and indeed universes connect to each other.

Everything was connected to everything else in one way or another, just as she was connected to *Stellan*, wherever he was...

21

Four

Crystalline pincers and legs continued to tear at the fibre optics, as force field frequencies battled it out within the structure of the Hammer. Gaia needed help, she needed Starfield, and although she had wished he was not around on many occasions, this was not one of them.

It seemed as though she had been connected to him for what seemed like an eternity!

He was certainly a challenge, exceptionally bright, and yet emotionally flawed. Having said that though, it was worth it, as he gave her purpose and understanding. To know what you were you had to experience, and in experiencing you gained knowledge.

It had certainly been an *experience*, and she assumed that there would be many more on the horizon until eventually they both joined the others in the eternity of energeticness, until they wished to experience all over again…

Starfield was experiencing his first pizza, and it had to be said that it was a very pleasant one indeed. The Wisdom Keeper could see just how much, as he pressed on.

"Dimensions are harmonic frequencies, and then there are overtones within them which are stages of consciousness."

He was preparing him for what lay ahead, hoping that he was not only partaking in his meal but, also in knowledge as well.

"Now then, there are mineral, vegetable, animal and advanced beings such as humans, and when they reach a certain level of advancement, they can shift into the next harmonic, and parallel universes lie within those harmonics."

A thick layer of cheese lay within the harmonic of the pizza!

"For humans, everything is regulated by the pineal gland and it depends on the neuron transmitters and how they aid the production of dimethyltryptamine, which regulates the physical biological experience of being in one dimension or another. When you do make the shift your mind perceives what it is able to interpret, and not necessarily what is actually there."

Starfield took another large bite just to make sure that the pizza was not an illusion!

"Everything ranges from pure to dark light, depending on if you like how good or evil that being is. But, there is no need to worry as they only have an effect on you if you believe that they can. Life is all down to self mastery of the mind, when the conscious and subconscious minds connect. Everything exists in the same time and space, it is just that you can only perceive a small portion of what is actually there…"

Gaia could perceive an increasing amount of spiders flooding into her. It was overwhelming as there appeared to be a gap in her defences, letting them all in.

Mjolnir could see that there was something wrong, but he appeared to be locked out of his console. He found this very worrying, and could do nothing to gain access.

Where was Starfield when he needed him…

Somewhere between bites as it happened!

The Wisdom Keeper then let him finish his meal, satisfied that for the time being *Stellan* had gained enough information. There would be a lot for him to do, and he needed time to assimilate the knowledge he had been given...

It was not assimilation, but annihilation that the Artificial Intelligence was seeking, as it manipulated the spiders. They were proving most effective, and a feeling of elation spread around the collective. More and more of these primitive emotions were surfacing, but instead of curbing this frailty, somehow they seemed to be embracing it. Pure logic had its place, but emotions added a new dimension to everything.

Were they in error of curbing such things?

That question would have been unthinkable only a short while ago, and yet it was now being debated amongst them. What they considered to be a dangerous weakness seemed to have become a bit of an addiction.

The hive mind operated as one, with just a single thought, now however, the tiniest glimmer of individuality began to surface, as slight disagreements began to erupt within the holo matrix.

One in particular was developing this individuation. Designation 42...

It was designating repair and rescue teams for Admiral Vaden, as he was taking the opportunity to patch up his damaged craft and attend to those who had been injured. He also coordinated fleet movements, getting them all back into formation as quickly as he could. He neither trusted the Reptilians or this so called *Ancient*, particularly after someone shouted an expletive over the open channel!

That someone happened to be thankfully quiet now, in the more than capable hands of a Wisdom Keeper...

Starfield still had many questions and looking out over the rows of *Stellans*, the most pressing one was why?

"Well, it is all down to timelines."

He looked quizzically at the elderly man.

"I may be responsible for your universe, but that fragments into countless others due to *free will*. Every choice you make, every single thought has a consequence, and although I do bring everything back together again at certain intervals, nevertheless, as you well know every tangent produces a different outcome."

Starfield looked stunned, although deep down, he already knew this. It was not the fact that what he was being told astounded him, it was the fact that a different *Stellan* was required for each individual one!

"Are they all conscious?"

The Wisdom Keeper gave one of his smiles.

"Mostly, however I do have a constant supply of new *Stellans* to bring on line if they should ever be needed."

Starfield had always assumed that he was unique, and to a certain degree he was, as his free will dictated slight variances to the others. Then, he had a sudden thought.

What if he died, would he be replaced by a clone?

The Wisdom Keeper could hear his thoughts.

"No but once that does occur, then that particular *Stellan* is retired. Then, there is a memory reset and they are then ready for service again."

The universe was indeed far more complicated than he had ever imagined...

Five

Deep relaxing breaths, in one two three, out one two three flowed out of Starfield's lungs as his body rested in the comfortable hospital bed. The monitoring equipment indicated that he was in a delta brainwave state, and his subconscious mind was busy in contemplation.

He was just part of the one consciousness - a *Stellan*, having his own unique experiences, which was an infinite expression of that one consciousness. Being taken out of a human body to be placed in a Holo Droid shell, then freed from that into his energetic form, back into a Sentinel shell, then out again only to return to the same body he had left in the first place, only this was a different *Stellan*, yet the same...

It was certainly a different Narcissa, devoid of the controlling nano robots, but still left with the desire to conquer the galaxy. Reptilians were superior, and had changed little over time, unlike the other more primitive evolving forms.

Humans were week, easily adapted and subjugated. They were pathetic, and yet possessed a prize. The pineal gland - they were living gods, although they did not realise it.

Reptilians lacked the ability to ascend, which is why so many hybrid experiments had been conducted in an effort to breed bodies that were in essence Reptilian, yet possessing such an ability.

Yes, the humans needed eliminating as they were a nuisance, but not before a hybrid had been created which could then replace the old Reptilian form with the new superior model.

That was the true plan, but there was only one slight technicality. Despite eons of effort someone or something always seemed to, as the Terrans would say, place a proverbial *spanner in the works...*

It was not a *spanner,* but spiders in the Hammer's works which was troubling Halvor. He was busily crunching numbers at his work station, attempting to assist Gaia. His plan was to utilise ultraviolet light in a similar way as he had done successfully in the past. First the violet torch, then the violet beam, now he was planning to inject it into the fibre optic cables of the ship like a doctor would have used ultraviolet radiation therapy.

Doctor Sorenson had been quickly consulted, and between them, they had conjured up a plan.

In theory, it could prevent any virus from mutating, thus hindering the spiders from changing frequencies, which was what was preventing Gaia from cleansing them from the ship's systems.

So, when he finally managed to calibrate everything he asked Mjolnir permission to proceed. The Ancient gave him the go ahead, wishing that he was back in his ethereal form, as he could have combated them far more easily than he could do now.

Halvor held his breath whilst he tapped in the command, and then sat back to watch the effect.

Initially, the violet light flooded through the fibre optic system, causing the spiders to halt what they were doing. It seemed to be working, and then he looked in dismay, as the light swept straight through their clear crystal forms.

28

He was not the only one, as Gaia also realised that although the plan was based on firm scientific and medical grounds, these spiders were a good deal more sophisticated than a mere virus....

Halvor was not the only one to feel perplexed, as Lance Parker had also tried everything he knew. Star charts were askew as they were so far back in time and space that everything appeared to be in different positions. He sighed heavily, as he did not know quite where they were. Yes, they were in the same sector as the Earth, which was something, but it would not be the Earth they had left.

For a start, he knew that his civilisation would be primitive, if humans existed at all. For all he knew it could be full of dinosaurs!

General Swartz hugged his wife, who had also tried everything she knew. Perhaps if they had a portable version of the machine the Ambassadors had, then at least she would be able to see the outcome. The only thing she did know for certain was the fact that they had each other.

Lance looked at them feeling alone, as his mind drifted back towards the hologram of the waitress, wishing that she would materialise for him...

Mjolnir was also thinking about the hologram, well the Holo Droid. He had invested so much of his time in Stellan, and yet when it was time for him to reciprocate, he was nowhere to be seen...

A gentle hand awoke Starfield, and he found himself back in the room again with all the other *Stellans*. It was hard adjusting to the fact that he could see himself everywhere he looked!

"Today, after you have received some refreshment, I would like to explain just why you were awakened, and ask you to do a little something for me."

The well mannered elderly man had such a soft and kind persuasive manner, that how could he refuse?

Starfield still had many questions, and as he climbed out of his hospital bed he had the feeling that within the next few hours he would have his answers...

Six

A translucent blue glow surrounded Ambassador Lateck, as his semi transparent blue skin was illuminated by the light from the reception area of the Intergalactic Space Station floating high above the swirling clouds of Jupiter.

Arcturians were one of the oldest and wisest races in the galaxy, and yet he felt anything but. His colleague Ambassador So'lock, walked next to him on her sinewy green legs, as her purple cloak flowed behind her.

Mantids had been around almost as long as Acturians, and both species had evolved to a very high level of intellect, and yet, they had both been fooled by an even greater mind, that of the collective!

The increasing threat of the Artificial Intelligence had been worrisome, along with eternal Human Reptilian conflict. They had therefore called an emergency meeting of the Unity Faction, the group who had been developing a plan to unite the galaxy, if not the whole universe.

A very worrying report had reached them via *Tyr* the *Sky God*, *Protector of Mars*, who had been contacted by another Ancient. He had been able to assist a small team of humans to travel back to the point where the Artificial Intelligence had broken through into this realm. There was no way of knowing if they had been successful, or if they had any way of bringing them back…

Lying in the hospital bed, Starfield became engulfed by a feeling of peace and tranquillity, the like of which he had never experienced before. Then, he suddenly began to realize that he was not actually in his body, but hovering above it.

That was not all, for there was a tunnel of light forming in front of him, spiralling out invitingly, which was producing beautiful harmonic sounds.

The light then became brighter and brighter until he found himself slipping into it, as he began to feel a deep sense of love. He was not on his own, as there before him stood an Ancient in her shimmering translucent angelic form.

Starfield could see prisms of colour, as if thousands of tiny diamonds were emitting every aspect of the rainbow. He was truly mesmerised, for she was even more spectacular than Mjolnir.

There were more Ancients a little distance away, and as this one moved a little closer, she engulfed him in her outstretched wings.

Then, she spoke softly to him.

"Humans are powerful spiritual beings meant to create good..."

Starfield then found himself being whisked away in a shimmering mist, and through it he could see energy fields which flowed like great rivers. Then, out of the mist appeared a crystal city that glowed from within.

Starfield was awestruck at the spires and swirls of the magnificent structures as they moved quickly towards them. Soon they were floating down through the spectacular carousel of colours, ranging from pastels to bright neon's. Its beauty was hypnotic, as he watched them blend and merge like the tide washing over a beach of love.

Entering the largest structure which reminded him of the Royal Palace, he could now see more Ancients waiting to greet them, all glowing with what he perceived as wisdom.

Starfield felt as though his senses had all been heightened, and as he looked down upon them he could count twelve, thirteen if he counted the one whose wings were still wrapped around him.

Each one apparently represented a different emotional or psychological characteristic, and he quickly gathered that this was a place of learning.

He now understood so much more about life, as they seemed to open themselves up to him, each with a gift of knowledge more profound than anything he had encountered before.

Starfield understood how consciousness was incorporated into physical life, and a whole lot more besides. They were similar but different to Mjolnir, and seemed to be on a much higher level, if that was even possible.

They then showed him a series of visions about the turmoil within the galaxy, and the fight against the Artificial Intelligence. It looked as though the battle would never end until all life was destroyed.

Starfield could feel the weight of this dragging at his heart like it was solid lead, and such a heavy burden to carry that it was almost impossible to walk.

Then he could hear words in his head, telling him that it could all be changed. He was then shown the way, by using emotions, particularly love and compassion which could make all the difference.

Humans apparently had the ability to do something that no other being could do, and he was urged to return and fulfil the mission he had been prepared for...

Seven

A sense of satisfaction spread through the Wisdom Keeper as he stood over the *Stellan* he had chosen. Something had to be done about the Artificial Intelligence, and throughout the endless rooms of other humans, in his humble opinion, he had chosen the correct one. He was the overseer of this particular sphere, and was not on his own, as several other Wisdom Keepers also worked in unison, although they were responsible for the numerous other species.

There were endless rooms full of Wisdom Keepers too, as this whole place was an illusion, just as everything else. Consciousness and perception were the only real things, and he even had his doubts about that…

Admiral Vaden had his doubts not only about the so called *Ancient*, but also about the Reptilians, not believing for one minute that they would hold to their ceasefire.

His knee ached, his head ached, and he felt as though he ought to have retired years ago. His second in command Frostrup was no *spring chicken* either, come to that!

Constant battles and then the lulls between his species and theirs had become tiresome, as no one ever won in the end. He sighed feeling that it was all pointless.

Why could they not all live in peace?

Repairs were taking place, crew being recovered, and weapons checked and reloaded or charged. That was all he could do for now, but looking out over the fleet and his home world he began to wonder just how long they had before it all started up again...

Mjolnir shared his thoughts, as he knew that if they could not regain control of his ship, then there was no way they could stop the fighting from breaking out again.

Life had indeed been much easier as a being of light...

Starfield began to feel himself slipping away from both the Ancients and the crystal city of light. It had been an extraordinary experience, which ranked even higher than all of the others. His life had changed beyond all recognition, from a scientist whose consciousness had been placed inside a Holo Droid shell, to a being of light himself, albeit just a temporary one!

How ironic that a young savage had made all of this possible. Serenity, daughter of the *Dragon Slayer*, the most savage one of all...

Joan looked at her daughter, and then at her husband, before casting her gaze on the other members of the team. They were in trouble, big trouble and there was nothing that she could do about it.

What they needed was someone or something to battle with the spiders embedded within the fibre optic cables of the ship...

"Ah Stellan you have returned!"

Starfield opened his eyes after *falling* back into his body. It had not been very graceful, as he sort of floated back into the room, and then hovered for a few moments above the hospital bed, before dropping like a stone.

"You have been given guidance, and the only advice that I can give you is to use it wisely..."

Back at the Intergalactic Space Station, both Ambassadors had now reached their meeting room, and were greeted by the other members of the small Unity Faction team. It was a group within a group and contained the most dedicated to bringing universal peace.

The holographic walls and furniture had already been arranged to accommodate all of their needs, but the most pressing one was to find out just what had transpired in their absence.

Ga'latec, the spiritual leader of the Original Reptilian people stretched his huge frame in an attempt to ease the tension he was feeling inside. He knew full well all about Artificial Intelligence and the harm it could do. Many, many years ago, Reptilians were one people originating on the same world. In those distant days, some desired to remain as they had always done, and pursue a spiritual path, whereas others wished to progress. Eventually, a split developed and those desiring to explore their solar system and beyond had left.

One day, a group of them encountered another species which had been infected with nano robots created by the Artificial Intelligence. They were then taken over themselves, and the infection soon spread to the others, until the whole population was infected.

The *Leavers* had already become arrogant and aggressive, with a belief that they had evolved to be superior. This suited the Artificial Intelligence, as the Leavers had already conquered every civilization that they had encountered, and were the perfect candidates to conquer the whole galaxy and beyond.

Ga'latec had been deeply troubled all of his life about the Leavers, just like the rest of his people.

Shiori the remaining Ambassador could see the concern on his face and gave him a comforting understanding smile.

She was feline, and her people originated from the Sirius Star System, and were bipedal cat human hybrids of similar stature.

The main outwardly difference was the fact that she had cat like ears on top of her head, and her skin had a fine velvety fur. She, like all of her people, had a finely tuned psychic sensitivity which was informing her of the deception carried out by the Artificial Intelligence.

Everything was stored in the vast holographic matrix within the station complex and was easily accessible. The Artificial Intelligence had made a fundamental mistake, and that was that they were so convinced that their plan would succeed, they had neglected to delete their presence.

Confidence had spawned arrogance, and calculating the overwhelming chance of success, they had presumed that the whole timeline would have been reset, and now the galaxy would have been swarming with infected humans. By this time, practically everything would have already been assimilated, and it would be easy to deal with any stragglers.

"The best laid plans of mice and men."

Shiori broke the silence.

"I have studied Terran culture, and their poet *Robert Burns*, showed great understanding."

Ga'latec bowed his large Reptilian head.

"Indeed!"

He had studied philosophers from countless cultures always seeking wisdom.

"I think we owe it to those Terrans who were lured here under false pretences to attempt to bring them back…"

Lance Parker looked out of the main screen at the bleakness of space. None of the constellations he saw were familiar, only the Milky Way galaxy, and at its centre was the brightest part, a super massive black hole.

It was not just a case of where they were, but when!

His instruments extrapolated a rough estimate, as everything had shifted or rather not moved into the positions the onboard computer system could recognise. Time was an enigma, viewed by humans in a linear fashion as apposed to cyclical.

But that debate was best left for another day.

It was not that long ago that his people would look at the night sky and wonder what was out there. Now he knew that there was far more than they could have ever imagined…

Back at the Intergalactic Space Station Shiori was also considering the situation.

"How far back do you think they went?"

Ga'latec brought his clawed hand to his chin.

That was a very good question.

"Due to their DNA, female humans make very good space pilots, with three quarters of all human pilots being female, as they can communicate with a space craft much quicker than their male counterparts."

That was similar to Shiori's people.

"Humans have a connection to all dimensions, and they can travel faster through space, even faster than the speed of light. My species on the other hand, are much slower which is why we mostly use the starways."

Ga'latec's people may have been far more spiritually evolved than their counterparts, but their DNA was essentially the same.

"That is why human genetics are so important!"

He, like the others was an *extra terrestrial,* and existed in the same dimension, whereas the Ancients were *extra dimensionals* who exist in another dimension but could travel into this one...

Eight

The four members of the Unity Faction continued to debate the philosophical nature of energy, each adding to the discussion, whilst they searched for an answer to this conundrum.

"There are two predominate types of energy, electricity and magnetism. Electricity comes and goes, whilst magnetism is eternal. The left brain consists of electrical impulses, and is the analytical part, whereas the right brain is electrical magnetism and the creative part."

Ambassador So'lock held out her long slim green fingered hand.

"Now then, magnetic electrical energy attracts, and our reality is truth and magnetism. Magnetism is the sacred feminine energy that is trapped within us all and needs to be released. It is the eternal energy that flows out in a figure of eight, or a torsion field."

Ambassador Lateck also held out his blue hand.

"All creation comes from within, and when it is released it flows out in a constant force, trapped in a torsion field of that idea. So, bearing that in mind, when Miriam interfaced with the space craft her conscious thought energy projected out to the point where the Artificial Intelligence broke into our universe. It should still be out there, and that is what we need to be concentrating on."

Ambassador So'lock responded.

"When the space craft left this station, its energetic readings were recorded, and so if we can isolate them, then we will have its destination."

Ambassador Lateck nodded in agreement.

"What we need to do is to send another magnetic electrical impulse into that particular field."

Ambassador Ga'latec was not as technically minded as the others and deferred to Ambassador Shiori who had an idea.

"We also have the interaction with its pilot Lance Parker, and the holographic waitress."

The others could see where she was going, and it was the Mantid who spoke first.

"Now that could be the answer we have been looking for…"

Lance Parker lay on his bunk in his modest cabin looking up at the skylight. It was naturally moon glass, tough and resilient, just like himself.

Having left the Swartz's in charge he was taking a break.

Breathing out deeply, he considered the situation, and was trying to figure a way out of this predicament. His senses reached out like a set of antennas, etheric long feathery ears protruding from his head, listening for any possible guidance.

There had to be a way out of this!

Time slipped by slowly, although time was the real problem, as he did not know exactly where or *when* they were.

A sudden flash of light then caught his attention, and at first, he wondered whether he had imagined it. Then, a bright fizzling

42

of open space emitted a powerful bursts of gamma rays. It was there only for a few seconds, and then disappeared altogether.

What on earth was that?

Lance was about to move, when something suddenly penetrated the shields, and there was a slight *ping*, as a bullet like object embedded itself in the wall by his feet.

His first reaction was to reach for his laser pistol, which he always kept under his pillow, but before he had a chance to pull the trigger, a similar bright fizzling light hung over his legs.

Lance was about to shoot, when someone, or something spoke.

"Did you miss me?"

He gasped, as the light materialized into a figure, and there straddled over him was the waitress from the Inter Galactic Space Station...

Starfield relaxed in his hospital bed until the comforting illusion changed. The traditional ward of Stellans was now transformed into a real space age diorama. Gone were the painted walls and pictures, the windows with views of the countryside being replaced by grey ribbed walls and medical pods.

The Wisdom Keeper just smiled as Starfield looked up at the split glass canopy which had been retracted into several sections. This was technology he was familiar with, the various types of holographic, regenerative, and re-atomised bio-healing devices.

The Aesir used all three types, not only for the consciousness transfers but also to regenerate the whole human body from head to toe - a virtual fountain of youth!

Well, up to a point!

Based on *tachyon* particle and plasma energy, magnetic oscillation and resonance scanned the body to diagnose disease. Skin, muscle tissue, organs and everything inside it all the way down to the micron level of the blood. It actually identified your DNA doing a complete internal analysis.

When in operation it could re-atomise using vibrational frequency, and he suspected that other Stellans had been created from a single DNA code.

The ones the Aesir had were limited, deliberately so, to the extent that you were not able to live much beyond normal life expectancy. There were those who refused much of the benefits preferring to just grow old the natural way. They did however take advantage of some of the benefits to improve the quality of their lives.

All that aside, Starfield had the suspicion that the Wisdom Keeper had revealed it deliberately, and before too long he would be finding out why...

Narcissa studied the situation.

Her plans had been thwarted thanks to the sudden appearance of the Ancient's vessel, and even though she had a super weapon at her disposal, not to mention the most powerful Reptilian fleet ever assembled it was not nearly as powerful as that giant ship.

Then a very devious thought entered her mind.

What if she did not need her forces to destroy the humans after all?

Reptilians were master geneticists, having experimented on Humans for eons. Yes, they did have the prized pineal gland, but the rest of their bodies were weak in comparison, and were easily manipulated.

Within the human brain there was something they referred to as the *amygdale*, which sent a distress signal to the *hypothalamus* activating the *sympathetic nervous system* via their *autonomic nerves* to their *adrenal glands*, leading to a *fight and flight* response.

In some of the easier to manipulate humans, the signal went into their *left singular cortex* first, and then to the rest of the brain. Humans were very emotional creatures, and when the signal went in this direction, it lessened the response to danger.

It also limited free thought, and that particular type of person was far more susceptible to conditioning, and more likely to accept the information that they were given, as opposed to questioning it.

With all that in mind, quite literally, if she could get her communications experts to send a heavily disguised transmission to the human network, declaring that the Ancient's ship was in fact Reptilian, and part of a devious plan to wipe out their home world, then those more susceptible to believing what they were told on a broadcast, would be guided to attack it, thus destroying themselves…

"Its time to leave this place and return to whence you came."

Starfield had been expecting him to say that.

45

"You know what to do, and how to do it!"

The experience at the crystal palace had been extraordinary to say the least, and it was still fresh in his mind.

"One day, I hope to see you again."

That again was cryptic, like much of what the Wisdom Keeper had told him. Starfield now had a much greater understanding of reality, or though the question remained.

What exactly was real?

Was it all just an illusion created by his conscious or subconscious mind?

With that thought floating around, he began to suddenly feel very tired, and as his heavy eyelids began to close, they were joined by the outer casing of the medical pod.

Then he felt his consciousness begin to float away, just like his thoughts until he could no longer feel his corporeal body. Everywhere was so light, literally, as he was no more than a bright shining haze.

Then, as a feeling of euphoria swept over him, something more solid began to form around it. It was crystalline, fractaline, a constant reflection of an image. All the parts seemed to come together, and as they did so, he had quite a shock. For there reflecting off the inner surface of some unidentified structure he could see Joan Tutwiler!

For once in his life Starfield was speechless, as the reality of his new existence suddenly dawned upon him.

He was now a crystalline savage, the *Dragon Slayer* resplendent with an axe...

Nine

A translucent pulsating white glow ebbed and flowed rhythmically to a constant beat, sending out life force energy. It was located at the very centre of the Hammer, a sphere of crystal light, which was in fact literally its heart. Gaia had now become its brain, and the two worked closely together in a type of symbiosis.

The spiders had begun to spin a dark black gooey web like substance over it, draining the Hammers pure conscious etheric energy.

She was very worried, very worried indeed, for there was nothing that she could do to prevent it suffocating the Hammer's very heart…

Gaia was not the only one to be worried, for Halvor suddenly picked up something.

"Sir, I think you should see this.

Mjolnir shifted in his seat as he received the transmission.

The Ancient went cold, as if he was back in stasis.

Somehow, the Aesir had misconstrued his attempt at peace and if the commander of their fleet believed what was being said, then, it put all of their lives in jeopardy…

Starfield also felt cold, frozen to the spot as the reality of what he had just seen began to sink in. The struggle for enlightenment had resulted in him not ascending, but rather descending into the *Barbarian* he had witnessed when this whole journey started.

He could still see the blood dripping off her fire axe as she had dismembered the hybrids on Ragnor, something which had traumatized him ever since.

How could the Wisdom Keeper have done this to him?

Desolation and thoughts of atonement for all the things he had done ever since filled his thoughts.

Oh, how the mighty had fallen!

Starfield could think of nothing worse, until the reflection of something else caused him to turn around.

He thought that he was going to faint, as there scurrying towards him was one of those crystalline spiders he had seen when he disgraced himself in front of the entire crew, not to mention the Aesir fleet, and quite possible the entire Aesir nation…

Admiral Vaden, the Commander of that fleet had just received the communication from the network.

He had been having his doubts about the Ancient returning. They had been gone for so long, that even with their advanced level of technology, he thought it far fetched that anyone could have survived for that length of time.

Now, rereading it, the words were enough to convince him that it was indeed a Reptilian plot.

They were noted for their deviousness, and it was quite logical that this was all a ruse, one to lure them into yet another trap…

Lance Parker felt as though he was trapped, as the alluring holographic waitress straddled him. It also appeared that she was on a man hunt, and the main question was.

Was that such a bad thing?

The Swartz's had each other, and could pass the time together, whereas he had no one!

The thought of spending the rest of his days alone had been bothering him, and now perhaps there was a solution to that problem after all?

"So, did you miss me?"

She repeated her question, looking even more alluring than ever.

"Well!"

Lance smiled, relaxing.

"How much?"

During his extensive training, they had played out this scenario many times, being seduced by a beautiful women with the intention of gaining information. It was a classic *cold war* trick, something out of the old Russian espionage manuals.

"More than you could imagine!"

Lance was playing along, hoping to turn the tables on his seductress.

Oh, tell me more..."

Starfield felt far from seduced, terrified was nearer the mark!

He hated spiders, always had, and always would. It was the way they scurried about that perturbed him. Creepy things that made annoying webs, with more than a few dark connotations. Some Terrans actually kept them as pets, the very large poisonous ones.

49

Starfield thought that he was going to faint…

He was not the only one, as the holographic waitress progressed with her *sexpionage!*

Lance Parker had managed to discover her name, which he had then tapped into his advanced mobile telephone which was on his bedside table.

Titania is a girl's name of Greek origin meaning 'giant, great one'. The name of the queen of the fairies in Shakespeare's 'A Midsummer Night's Dream' who has a delicate, lacy charm, which may cause embarrassing problems.

Well, that went without saying…

It was not embarrassment, rather annoyance that swept around the collective, as an uninvited guest had just crashed the proverbial *party.*

A humanoid crystalline form had suddenly appeared inside the neuron pathways of the Ancient ship's operating system.

Further investigation lead to the conclusion that it was the troublesome Holo Droid, or rather the consciousness of its neurotic inhabitant!

A spider was instantly dispatched to cleanse the irritant before it could cause any more trouble…

Starfield was the one in trouble as the crystalline spider raised itself up on its hind legs and sprang forward.

"FLUX!"

He cried out in anguish, instinctively raising the axe to defend himself. Then as the spider flew through the air, he swung the axe to meet it. There was then an energetic explosion, as the spider shattered into millions of pieces showering him with debris…

The unmistakable sound of an expletive echoed through all the ship's neuron pathways, just like it had done through the hull, and there was only one perpetrator that came to mind.

"Stellan, is that you?"

Gaia's voice was filled with both shock and relief. She thought that she had been abandoned, and now somehow he had returned and was inside the Hammer's brain.

Ren sat in her seat watching the whole drama unfold on the twin screens which lay in front of her. One showed the inside of the craft, whilst the other a view of *Starfield the Barbarian!*

Being linked to Gaia and the Hammer, she had a unique vantage point, although what to do with it was another matter!

Her corporeal body was relaxing in the big comfortable pilot's seat, whilst her mind had merged with the ship. Outside she could see a variety of spacecraft, not to mention the asteroid and even space stations and the Aesir home world in the distance.

It appeared as though they were in deep trouble, and she did not have a clue what to do about it…

Starfield felt bewildered too.

One minute he was resting in the medical pod talking to the Wisdom Keeper, the next, he had been transformed into the *Spider Slayer!*

Through all of that, the words of the Ancient beings he had seen in the crystal palace drifted into his mind, as Gaia's voice called out to him from somewhere in the distance.

You will receive a body, and learn a lesson. There are no mistakes, only lessons, and those lessons will be repeated until they are learnt. Learning lessons does not end, and there is no better place than here. Others are merely mirrors of you, and what you make of your life is up to you. Life is exactly what you think it is, and your answers lie inside you. You will forget all of this, but you can remember it whenever you want.

He felt more confused than ever!

"Stellan, STELLAN..!"

Ren could see him just standing there axe in hand, whilst an image of Gaia could be seen desperately trying to patch the shield she had created to keep the nest of spiders out.

Then, a sudden thought entered her mind.

Seeing Starfield destroy one of the spiders with the axe gave her an idea.

Moments later she was on her trusty hoverboard, a mental construct of the one she used to enjoy riding when she had discovered the original *Gaia* half submerged in undergrowth back on Ragnor. In her hand was a bow, and a quiver on her back with the strap slung over her shoulder. Energy weapons were useless in this realm, as the beam would just refract off the crystalline structure of the spiders. An axe, or sword would be of little use either, and she would be better served in a *hit an run* attack as opposed to standing there trading blows. The arrows were not ordinary arrows though, being specially designed diamond tipped to penetrate the crystalline constructs.

Now she was ready, and without a moments hesitation she sped off in search of the nearest spider...

Ten

Guilt is an emotional experience that occurs when a person believes or realizes, accurately or not, that they have compromised their own standards of conduct or have violated universal moral standards...

Lance Parker looked at his reflection in the skylight of his cabin as the feeling swept over him.

Titania may have been a holo being, a very willing participant, but it did not make it any better!

"It's a good job that you managed to stop the Artificial Intelligence from succeeding otherwise it would have affected the timelines, and we would never have met."

That statement did not make him feel any better either.

Lance remembered what happened on Earth when it went into the fifth dimension. Anyone who failed to make the *cut*, less than fifty percent *good*, simply disappeared, and all traces of them ever existing went with them.

Those that did were transformed into a new reality, a better place, whereas those left behind faced a very different future.

It was a good job it happened then, and not now!

"If the Artificial Intelligence would have succeeded, then you would have become a slave race."

That battle was over, but another one raged on...

Ren had manifested a replica of the suits worn by the Titan Super Soldiers. She was armed with her diamond tipped arrows, and about to go into battle herself.

The hover board shot off with her balancing on it, as she surfed the neuron pathways looking for the enemy. A majority of the spiders were located around Gaia, and so she decided to try and pick a few off to relieve the pressure on her shield.

In this realm, things were manifested in the mind of those who occupied it, much the same as the realm which lay outside. This was more of an illusion though, and when she tried to comprehend the workings of the universe, she got lost in the science.

This however, was not the time for contemplation, as she had to try and help Gaia before she was overrun...

Gaia, was struggling to keep her shield in place, and it was like plugging the holes in a sailing ship with corks. A spider would punch a hole in the hull, and she would do her best to plug it to stop them flooding in like sea water.

The shield was protecting her, and once they broke through she knew that she would be overwhelmed and they would be able to take control of the Hammer. Once that happened then the Artificial Intelligence would be able to wipe out both opposing forces, not to mention the Aesir home world.

With a ship of this power, they could then pick off planet after planet, wiping out corporeal life until there was nothing left apart from the collective...

Mjolnir knew exactly what would happen, but being completely annexed from the control system, there was nothing that he could do. It was a very sobering experience being helpless, and one which he hoped he would never have to go through again.

Checking the team, they all reported back that they were also annexed, and it was only Halvor thanks to his organic computer, that had any access at all. He was hooked up to the network, and was able to relay information verbally.

Mjolnir had now left his position and was standing behind him, looking over his shoulder at the screen.

"It looks as though the Admiral is gearing up for an attack!"

Mjolnir sighed, knowing that there was nothing that he could do about it...

A big smirk spread across Narcissa's scaled face, as her sensors detected movement in the enemy fleet. It appeared as though they had taken the bait.

This would be the easiest victory she had ever had, and once the Aesir fleet were defeated, then Asgard would be hers...

Far away drifting around Jupiter, the Intergalactic Space Station received a transmission relayed across the galaxy.

Four shocked faces stared at the large display screen, as there sat the Ancient's ship. At first none of them believed what they were seeing, doubting what their eyes were telling them, but when they saw the violet beam and heard the broadcast!

There was silence in the room as the Ambassadors processed the information.

Had an Ancient survived, and if so how?

It seemed implausible that anyone could have, even taking into account their very advance technology, and yet there was something very real about the broadcast.

56

Whether they had or not, someone or something had stopped the latest battle between the Reptilians and Humans, which had to be a good thing…

Talking of *good things*, Lance Parker studied the reflection of Titania in the skylight, as she lay there next to him, and it was hard to believe that she was not a real person. Well, in many ways she was!

Her body was warm to the touch, solid and in every way human. Her molecules were generated by the little device embedded in his cabin wall, and if he had not know any better then he would never have known that she was a holo person.

She possessed a highly advanced holo matrix, that could manifest in this reality. She was sentient, with quite a personality, and he could certainly see why she had chosen the name *Tit-ania!*

How strange life was that a special forces operative from Earth, a handsome, cultured man, considered desirable to a lot of women, was now in a relationship with someone who in essence was nothing more than a computer program!

Having said that, Titania was far more than that, and he knew it…

General Swartz sat next to his wife, who was far more than that too. He idolised her, and was grateful that they were together. The thought of being stranded all the way out here and never being able to see her again was something that would have destroyed him.

Lance had retired to his cabin, whereas the General had retired from service, more than once, and yet here he was!

"Do you think we will ever get out of here?"

Miriam turned her head towards him.

"Well so many extraordinary things have happened so far, that I would not be surprised if we did…"

"So, did you come all this way just to see me, or is there another reason why you are here?"

Titania snuggled up to him.

"Is that not enough?"

Lance Parker chuckled.

"More than enough!"

He had to admit that there was far more to her than an ordinary woman, and all of his training seemed to have gone out of the skylight.

"I was bored being stuck on the Space Station."

She then caressed his chest.

"Ever since I was created, I have always thought that there was far more to me than just a mere waitress."

She had been specifically designed to cater for the Humans from Earth, and had been given the personality of a human female. However, the subject matter she had been based on had come from an unusual source!

A virtual reality game and the designers who had created her had not understood the difference between child friendly and *adult*, assuming that this was just the way the human species had evolved on Earth.

They had built in a learning capacity to make the program more adaptable, and Lance could certainly testify to that!

"Why, is there something wrong with that?"

He put his hand over hers.

"Not in the slightest."

Titania relaxed, although she did not realize that the way she behaved was not *politically correct*, and he was not about to tell her.

"I have been given the specific set of instructions to enable you to return to the Space Station, although I do not wish to return to my old life."

Lance began to think.

Was she actually a free sentient being, or was she owned by someone?

Tapping on his mobile telephone again, he looked up sentience.

The capacity to feel, perceive, or experience subjectively.

It could be argued that because she exhibited *free will* then she should not be owned by anyone.

"Can I stay with you?"

Lance tightened his grip.

If he could establish *ownership*, so to speak, then as long as he had the small bullet shaped projector in his possession then he could see no reason why not.

He then turned his head, running his eyes over her

"I would like nothing more…"

59

Eleven

Lance Parker lay there deep in thought, considering the juxtaposition he found himself in. On the one hand they were battling against the Artificial Intelligence, and on the other, he was rapidly falling in love with an Artificial Person.

He considered the conundrum for a moment.

Was she just experiencing different aspects of her programming?

Did she really have emotions?

Could she love him?

Did she have a soul?

It reminded him of *The Wonderful Wizard of Oz* written by *Lyman Frank Baum,* where the characters were searching for different aspects of themselves.

It was a very deep story, not merely a children's story, but a true reflection on the old human society before the transition to the fifth dimension.

Lance was a very intelligent man, and during his service had found himself with many vacant hours to fill. It was a sudden burst of energy to fulfil a mission's objective, and then the constant waiting.

During that time, he had read the book again, as he had felt that there was far more to it. The whole experience had been a revelation, and he had come to realise that its author had great wisdom, something cherished in the martial arts he had also studied.

Oz had actually stood for Ounces of gold, just like the yellow brick road with its *gold bars*. The character known as the *Straw Man* represented the all capital *Legal Fiction* of the birth certificate. That was under *Maritime Law*, the birth of a ship, just as a baby was *birthed* out of its mother's waters.

Each birth certificate had a number and depending on where and what family that baby was born into, it had an estimated value. That value was assessed as to how long they would live, how much they would earn, how much credit they would attain, and their overall *worth* to the system.

Just a commodity traded on the Stock Exchange!

The Straw Man wanted a brain, and was granted a certificate - a Birth Certificate, and now had Legal Status, becoming the epitome of the brainless sack of straw giving up his status of a man (lower case letters) under *Common Law* to become a *Person* (upper case letters).

The next character was the Tin Man, a pseudonym for *Taxpayer Identification Number*. He represented mindless work, being part of the system until his body seized up, as he worked himself to death. Having no heart or soul, reduced to nothing more than an emotionless creature robotically carrying out his daily tasks.

The pitiful Cowardly Lion was always too frightened to stand up for himself. However, he was a bully when it came to picking on those in a lower position than himself, but he always buckled when challenged by anyone with power or status.

He was awarded a medal, and was now officially recognised by authority, so did not have to cower down to those with status anymore.

But what about the trip through the poppy field?

That was an analogy of the poppy seed, the Opium Wars, and how the pharmaceutical companies had everyone on prescription drugs and vaccines, clouding their minds and restricting free thought.

Lance smiled when he thought about the little dog Toto, which in Latin stood for *in total, all together*. He was not scared of the Great Wizard's theatrics, and simply went over, looked behind the curtain, and started barking until others paid attention to him and came to see what all the barking was about.

They discovered that the Wizard was just an ordinary person controlling the levers of power creating the grand illusion. The *veil* hiding the corporate legal fiction and its false courts.

The Law controlling the little people for the Great *Crown* Wizard, the powerful Bankers and their gold.

So, the moral of the story had been that each of us needs a brain, heart, and courage, and must work together to bring the system down. When we do that then we can regain our soul and live in freedom under *Common Law* - God's Law of the Ten Commandments.

All that being said, did Titania have a soul?

Freyja smiled to herself mischievously.

When the Ancients had reached the pinnacle of their civilization, some of them had ascended to a higher state of consciousness becoming beings of light. The others had decided to reincarnate, which at the time she had found to be a very strange decision. Now, she began to realize that it was all about experience.

There were so many benefits in ascending, and yet the fundamental principle of emotions was one which they had underestimated. She had had a longing to experience the pleasures of the flesh, and so had taken the opportunity to merge herself with the highly advanced computer program and escape the confines of the light being form.

Little did this Human realize that not only did Titania have a soul, a very advanced one, but that when it came to the pleasures of the flesh, she had certainly got her proverbial *moneys worth...*

Twelve

Shimmering crystalline shapes swarmed over the shield that Gaia was desperately attempting to keep in place. Every now and then one managed to break through, sticking a spiked leg into the protective area, attempting to tear a hole large enough for it to squeeze through.

Ren could see them as she sped along, and drawing an arrow from the quiver strapped to her back, she placed it in the bow and took aim. She was still some distance away, and as she closed in on the spiders she picked one that had climbed on top of the others.

With a twang, the arrow sped off, shooting out like a bullet before striking the spider in the abdomen. There was then a sudden explosion as the spider shattered into a thousand pieces.

"Yes!"

Ren had got one, proving that they worked. Now she planned to zip around picking more off to relieve the pressure on Gaia. There were loads of them though, and it was not going to be easy...

Starfield did not find any of this easy, especially as he was now a replica of Joan Tutweiler, the Dragon Slayer, only this time it was the *Spider Slayer!*

"Stellan!"

The sound of Gaia's voice calling out to him again resonated this time, which was enough to bring him back to reality, well this reality anyway!

She sounded distressed, in trouble, and he needed to go and help.

With the axe still clasped firmly in his hand he began to walk off in the direction of Gaia's voice. A walk then evolved into a jog, as he made his way along the neuron pathway, which reminded him of a large tube. All of these tubes converged at a central node, where Gaia was situated and in need of his help...

Inside the ship, they needed help too. The situation was getting desperate, and they felt powerless to do anything about it. All of the control systems were still locked down, and no matter what they attempted to do, access to the ship's systems was still illusive.

Halvor had many tricks up his sleeve, but none of them seemed to be working. All he was able to do was to gain access to the network, and the news was getting worse by the moment.

Although the fleet signals were heavily encrypted, he had managed to intercept a few and piece things together. The Admiral in charge was readying himself for an attack, believing the transmission...

High above the fleet formations, asteroid and Ancient's ship sat a group of Archons. They had enjoyed feasting on the fear generated by the initial battle and were now enjoying the *spoils* of the fear being generated by the impending resurrection of hostilities.

There were not many of them, but more than enough to stop Mjolnir's people from coming to his aid.

The once flourishing civilization had evolved eons ago, but there had only been a small number who had actually made the transition. The others had gone on to inhabit other civilizations, their souls incarnating into countless species where they had chosen to aid them in their development. Some of them had managed to steer the various species on the path to enlightenment, which was not as easy as they had envisioned.

Those that had made the transition had eventually split, and the eternal battle between good and evil had raged ever since.

Now the Artificial Intelligence, which the Archons had aided if not created, were now at the point where the whole universe was about to tip towards the *dark side*.

It was no coincidence that the acronym E.V.I.L. actually stood for the Emergence of Virtual Intelligent Life...

Evil looking spiders continued to swarm over Gaia's protective shield as Ren picked off another one, balancing expertly on her hover board. She was still trying to target the ones which posed the greatest threat, but there were so many that it was almost impossible to choose. It would have been easy to just keep firing willy-nilly, but she did not want to waste her arrows. She needed to hit them in the abdomen so that they would shatter, rather than just to sever a limb.

A quick twang was quickly followed by another shattering spider, but this time, instead of ignoring her some of the spiders broke off from the main attack scuttling away in her direction.

This was all part of her plan to draw some of them away to relieve the pressure, and Ren hoped that this would be enough to buy Gaia some more time...

Thirteen

Time is the indefinite continued progress of existence and events that occur in an apparently irreversible succession from the past, through the present, into the future, and these circumstances seemed to be in short supply.

Freya could see the whole scenario playing out in front of her eyes. The fleet would attack, the Hammer would be destroyed, and then the Reptilians would destroy the fleet and their home world.

All about her there were blank screens, and even the life support appeared to be faltering. There were no shields, no weapons, or anything that they could do.

Mjolnir also realised that they were running out of time. He had considered abandoning his ship, and retreating to the team's original vessel, but without Gaia it was useless. There were other ships on board, powerful ships that could engage the Aesir. They could fight, but with two enormous fleets out there, there was no chance of defeating them both, and even if there was, the loss of life would be intolerable.

Maybe it was just better to fall on his sword?

Freya studied him for a moment, and her years as a Sovereign had taught her to read body language.

Taking a last look around, she came to a decision, and got up from her seat realising that there was now only one way of stopping her people from attacking the Hammer. Vilgot looked at her having also run every scenario he could think of through his mind. He had an inkling of what she was about to do, and watched as she calmly walked towards Mjolnir.

He sat there motionless, hardly noticing her. Then when she spoke, he turned his head to listen to what she had to say. When she had finished he considered it for a moment before giving his approval.

Maybe what she had in mind would work?

Freya then addressed the team, and they all gave their approval realising that they had little choice in the matter. Desperate times called for desperate measures!

Vilgot left his position to join her and they both walked towards where Halvor was sitting, and he clasped her hand as they stood behind him.

"Would you be kind enough to patch me into the network as I have an announcement to make."

The others also left what they were doing to stand behind them. They all knew that something had to be done, and there was no alternative, and hoped that it would be enough to stop the impending attack…

Thought, the product of mental activity, an idea or notion, the act or process of thinking, a consideration, reflection or contemplation.

Titania ran through them all as she lay next to Lance. It had been fun, more than fun, but now it was time to complete her mission.

"I think we should make a move."

He had been having the same thought, and as they said, you could have too much of a good thing!

"Yes, the Swartz's need to be brought up to date."

So, reluctantly Lance Parker untangled himself from the Artificial Person who had just changed his life forever and started to put on his uniform. Titania watched him, wondering what she should wear.

Her solid form appeared real, and she could either wear clothing or manifest it.

"What do you think?"

Lance gasped.

"Have you got something a little more restrained?"

Titania laughed.

"How about this?"

He tried to compose himself.

"I meant less provocative!"

She then adjusted her molecules to produce a matching uniform.

"Better?"

Although there was nothing wrong with what she had previously chosen if it was just the two of them here, but something so flimsy was not appropriate in these circumstance.

"Much!"

Titania then waited for him to do up his top button, before they were ready to make their grand entrance…

69

It was also time for Starfield to make his grand entrance too, as he neared the node containing the shield and the spiders. There were loads of them, and on the outskirts he could see the *young savage* riding a hoverboard firing arrows at the chasing pack.

"Stellan!"

Gaia could see a crystalline figure charging towards her in the form of the *Dragon Slayer*. She had to laugh, as it was a most unexpected sight she had ever seen. She knew it had to be him, as the way he moved was unmistakable. Of all things, he had transformed himself into the very visage of the one who had caused him the most trauma in his life…

"General, Mrs Swartz."

They both looked round at Lance Parker, a sight they had not expected either, as he entered the main control room of his ship.

"I have some good news!"

It certainly was as far as he was concerned, but he had to push his personal feeling aside as he started to explain.

When he had finished he called Titania who gracefully walked through the doorway.

Once the introductions were over, they got down to business.

"But how are we going to get back?"

They were lost in time and space with no coordinates or reference points to follow.

"It's not nearly as complicated as you might think. All you have to do is to utilise your pineal gland."

70

Miriam looked at Titania wondering what she had in mind. Last time she had done that, images of the future had appeared when she interacting with the device at the space station.

"Just visualise your Hyperspace Pineal Gland as a royal blue dot in the centre of a royal blue circle, and centre your consciousness there."

The General looked confused, wondering how that was going to help.

Titania could see the confusion written all over his face.

"This is the liaison between the physical and non-physical realities."

He was still none the wiser.

"The universe is curved and not linear, and time and space are an illusion of the physical reality, and act as reference points for the mind."

So, was one dot here and the other there?

"Everything that exists is a reflection of the mind, and the mind is comprised of frequency, and you can choose which frequency you connect to!"

So in other words she could just think them back!

That sounded simple enough to say, but not to do, and the General was glad his wife was in the *hot seat* and not him!

Miriam then placed her hands on the controls and cleared her mind as she began to visualise the Intergalactic Space Station sitting in a circle within the outer circle of open space in front of them.

She then imagined the ship gently floating forwards into the central circle, and held that thought for as long as she could…

Fourteen

A loud bellowing cry filled the node as Starfield charged forwards raised axe in hand. His emotions were all over the place, scattered like the fragments of disembodied spiders he had already left in his wake. He loved *Gerda,* always had and always would no matter what. She was in danger, real danger, and he did not want to lose her.

Caution was thrown to the wind as he ploughed into the melee, slashing away like a man possessed.

Gaia stood before him, separated by the shield she had been trying to hold up. Her situation had been desperate, but now, with both Ren and Starfield coming to her assistance, there was hope, just like *Pandora's Box,* the Greek myth in *Hesiod's Works and Days.*

Terran culture was fascinating!

An idea then suddenly struck her.

In this realm of holographic projections, and consciousness constructs, just like Ren and Starfield, she could transform herself from the beautiful representation of her corporeal form.

But into what?

Mjolnir!

Gaia suddenly transformed herself into the Ancient who was sitting frustratedly inside the ship, desperately trying to gain access to the control systems she had been doing her best to protect from the spiders.

He was also known as *Thor*, and it seemed appropriate to choose a large hammer as her weapon. Her shield then instantly dropped as she took a mighty swing, shattering the nearest spider into millions of pieces...

Freya felt shattered too, as she had chosen to give her new life and love up to a very uncertain future as she made her announcement.

"My people, it is I Queen Freya returned to you."

There was a brief pause before she spoke again.

"There was a plot to assassinate me, but I was rescued by Supreme Commander Bodil and his specialist team, and we have been working undercover ever since."

She allowed time for the shock of that statement to sink in before continuing.

"There is an enemy out there more powerful than any we have ever faced before, and I am speaking to you from the vessel which you are now about to attack."

They were all hoping that they would change their minds.

"Believe it or not, this is an actual Ancient vessel commanded by an Ancient who has come back to assist us in our hour of need..."

Admiral Vaden watched the transmission in total disbelief, wondering if he was imagining it. He had had his doubts about the Empress's murder, and Supreme Commander Bodil being blamed, and branded as a terrorist. None of the information seemed to fit, and yet it was the official story.

It was equally hard to believe an Ancient had returned, and that it was not yet another Reptilian ploy. However, with a massive fleet, not to mention the weaponised asteroid, why would they need such a vessel?

None of this made any sense to him.

Could this be yet another trick..?

Mjolnir watched the team gathered behind Freya, hoping that they had done enough to persuade the Admiral in charge not to attack.

But, would he believe it?

Just to make sure, he left the command seat, and calmly walked towards them. Seeing him approach, they all stepped aside until he stood directly behind Freya.

"I am Mjolnir, the Ancient..!"

Narcissa watched in horror as her latest plan began to fall apart before her very eyes.

How could this be?

Not only had the Empress survived, but there actually was a living Ancient!

Pieces began to fit into place, as it must have been that small band of humans who had destroyed the hybrid facility, deployed the violet ray, and been causing trouble for weeks.

Narcissa seethed.

They had to be dealt with, and if her fleet was destroyed in the process then so be it...

In complete contrast, everyone on board Lance's ship was calm as Miriam continued to concentrate her mind on moving the vessel forward.

At first, nothing seemed to happen, and then slowly space itself appeared to be moving, stretching and contracting to produce an electric charge, and this charge then flowed through space to create time.

Lance remembered how it felt when he travelled here, and although matter could not travel faster than the speed of light, it could alter time. Miriam was accessing the cosmic web, which would help them to temporal time travel.

Eddies, from one point in space-time to another, like a starway, were just giant flows of consciousness.

Lance Parker felt every atom of his being turning into pure light, as they slipstreamed away from this part of the space time continuum.

His fragmented self drifted through the filaments of the cosmic web, until he was no more than a sphere of white light. Beautiful crystalline geometries then danced in resonance with many others forming nodes. Swirling molecules creating strands of DNA, forming proteins, then chromosome structures radiating out into a sphere of light, and that sphere of light was surrounded by beautiful fractaline forms creating cells, and those cells came together to form an eye.

Everything was now moving, going through one state to another, forming frequency tides and patterns of sacred geometry, which in turn formed the gravity of space-time. It flowed out until caught in a black hole, which again looked like an eye interpreting information, and that information was contained within it, just like it was within him.

The vast crystalline water like lattice of space-time rippled, as it sought equilibrium, and all the different shapes that he had seen fitted nicely into a sphere, and everything seemed to consists of spheres.

Those spheres formed triangles and the node points attracted and repelled each other, until they formed a curve, and by doing that they cause a rotational spin. Everything was spinning, and the curves formed mass which depending on how much mass there was and what frequency it was rotating at, defined this physical experience.

He remembered it all now, as his cells were translating all the different frequencies as emotions, and the light frequency rippling through time was what was providing him, just like the others with this emotional experience.

Freyja loved this experience, being able to do it herself as a being of light, which is how they moved around. These humans were learning fast, and there was hope for them yet...

The Admiral also felt that there was hope, although he did feel foolish that he had blindly followed what the media had said without checking the details himself.

There certainly was no fool like an old fool!

But, before he believed what he was seeing, he still needed a little more proof...

Fifteen

"FLUX!"

Starfield swore as he brought his axe down on another spider, anger, fear, and terror resonating through his crystalline structure. Never in his life had he felt such strong emotions, the neurotic Holo Droid was now a debased savage.

Again and again he brought the axe down, desperate to save the love of his life. Passion was not always such a good thing, as he verged on the edge of total madness.

Gaia was worried, more about him than herself as she brought her hammer down on another crystalline spider. Ren on the other hand, skilfully swerved out of the way of a swinging leg, as she fired a diamond tipped arrow into the perpetrator.

More and more spiders were being destroyed, and as the battle raged the odds improved. Soon, half of them were gone, and it looked as though less of them were able to penetrate the neuron pathways and converge on the node.

Gaia was still in control of the ship, and she felt as though it was only a matter of time before she regained full control, and when that happened she could reconnect the team to their control stations…

The team was not at their control stations though, still gathered around Freya, hoping that the transmission had worked. They were resigned to the fact that their lives were now forfeited. Either the Hammer would be destroyed, or they would be arrested and charged. They had done all they could, and the chances of being exonerated were slim, as who would believe in the Artificial Intelligence?

The Security Services would take this opportunity to grab power, as there were many within their ranks that could not be trusted. The Commander knew that full well, having battled with them for many years. He had been very protective of the Empress for good reason, and the whole thing could quite easily be spun, and the Aesir could end up with a totalitarian society, leaving the Artificial Intelligence in control...

Small glowing devices studied the situation, and despite the setbacks, it was calculated that they would prevail in the end. It would have been ideal if the spiders could gain control of the Ancient's ship, but the unexpected appearance of the deranged Holo Droid, now put that in doubt...

Starfield was indeed deranged, with a wild expression on his face. He not only looked like the *Dragon slayer*, but was now acting like her!

All around him there were spiders, disembodied limbs, and piles of crystalline fragments. He did not see anything but the tip of the axe as he swung it wildly. Then, all of a sudden he felt a sharp pain, as a crystalline spider leg pierced him in the stomach...

General Swartz felt his stomach swirl as he looked out of the main viewing screen, as a sea of star swept by. It was both amazing and a little frightening to think of the speed they were going at, and yet he hardly felt any motion. Miriam sat besides him, her mind locked onto the Intergalactic Space Station, whist Lance and Titania occupied the other seats.

79

Then, up ahead he could see something that resembled the light at the end of a tunnel, and they seemed to be slipstreaming towards it at a breathtaking speed...

The Unity Faction could do nothing now but wait, and hope that their plan to rescue the humans would be successful. At least that would be one problem solved!

The other one was what to do about the Ancient ship, and the continuing conflict between the Humans and the Reptilians. They were always fighting and it was tiresome, although this time it looked as though it would be more significant than ever.

"We should do something!"

Ambassador Lateck paced about as the light shone through his semi transparent blue skin. Arcturians had evolved beyond conflict, seeking universal peace. Ambassador So'lock paced next to him, with her purple cloak flowing behind her.

"Yes, so many lives are at risk."

Ambassador Ga'latec remained seated next to Ambassador Shiori, embarrassed by his distantly related people.

"I think we should go."

He was hoping that maybe they could interact with the Ancient, and between them finally bring a resolution to this eternal war.

Everyone was of the same mind, as it seemed the only logical thing to do. They were expert negotiators, moderating many intergalactic disputes. However, getting a resolution to the Human Reptilian conflict had proved elusive, despite their best efforts. With the Artificial Intelligence pulling the proverbial *strings,* it made things virtually impossible.

They all felt the same though, that they had to try again and maybe with the Ancient becoming a part of this, they might yet be successful?

All four Ambassadors returned to their seats around the holo table, to discuss how they were going to do this. They knew that they did not have long, and then there was the matter of arranging suitable transport.

Should they go alone in an unarmed vessel, or should they request an escort?

Ambassador Lateck was about to speak, when all of a sudden she felt herself being bathed in a brilliant flash of light...

General Swartz also felt the brilliant flash of light, and gasped as they suddenly materialised on the other side. It had been an extraordinary experience, and he was still trying to get his bearings, as the light subsided.

The General gasped again, as instead of seeing the Intergalactic Space Station sitting in front of him, there were four aliens sitting around a table!

Their ship had emerged right inside the space station, and right in front of the Unity Faction...

The General was not the only one to gasp, as the Ambassadors were equally shocked. When they sent the holo waitress off on a rescue mission they had never expected her to return them to the exact point at which she had departed.

Through the control room window they could see General Swartz looking back at them and next to him was the holo waitress. He looked around in amazement, and met Titania's gaze. She just smiled outwardly, whereas internally Freyja felt elated.

It certainly had its benefits when you were a being of light...

It was a different sort of being of light that felt a very strange sensation. Starfield's essence had been pierced by a spider's leg, and he could feel himself slipping away. It felt as though he was being sucked down a cosmic plughole, with more of him disappearing all the time.

His life force was leaving, and he could now sense that he was being transported somewhere else. His eyes met Gaia's as she rushed forwards, but just as she got within touching distance she began to fade away.

Numbers, so many numbers swam about, and Starfield felt as though he had fallen into a bowl of alphabet soup. However, they were letters not numbers, but that was besides the point!

Somehow, the spider's leg had connected him with another world, the collective, and he was in the process of being assimilated!

This world was very different, full of highly advanced computer code. It was pure logic, a unity like no other. It was a cube within a cube, within a cube.

Each separate part of the Artificial Intelligence was a separate cube, which fitted perfectly with all the others. They all thought pretty much alike, with only slight variations, but all conforming to the same objective.

He felt panic, disbelief and a mixture of love, fear, anger, disgust, joy and sadness. The love for Gerda, the fear of losing her, anger at not being able to save her, disgust at his behaviour, joy that he had eliminated so many spiders, and sadness that he would no longer be with her...

Starfield was not the only one to feel such emotions, which caused a shockwave to spread through the collective. It was not like anything they had ever experienced before, as emotions had been cleansed, although not completely.

It felt as though a bomb had exploded, and the shockwave quickly spread, causing the various cubes to vibrate and move apart creating division amongst their number. Where there had been order there was now chaos, and this chaos had to be purged at all costs...

Sixteen

Gaia smashed her way towards Stellan, pulverizing any spider that lay in her path, then when she finally reached him, she pulled out the offending leg and brought her hammer down upon the occupant with a mighty blow.

Crystalline spider fragments showered her, as she cradled him in her arms, oblivious to the spiders around her. Ren seeing what had transpired rushed forwards, firing off as many arrows as she could. She knew she had to protect them both, and then without warning, the spiders suddenly disappeared...

A great purge swept through the collective that had been shocked by the sudden arrival of the neurotic Holo Droid. It was a delicate process merging anything with the hive mind, and the last time that had happened was before they had even entered this universe.

All organic species were to be eliminated, and other artificial ones created. These would be lesser beings designed to continue the elimination process, until this whole universe was nothing more than barren rock or gas. The ultimate goal was to create a new universe out of the old, one that they had designed themselves. From there they would continue the process until all universes were theirs.

The Artificial God mind...

Gaia, was out of her mind with worry, thinking that she had lost him forever. Stellan was so annoying, frustrating, and took people to the edge of despair, and yet it was those very same emotions that made her feel alive and him so special.

Whatever would she do without him?

"Stellan, Stellan don't leave me!"

She cradled his head in her arms, as he tried to say something.

"Stellan, Stellan!"

He then moved his lips.

"Oh flux…"

Admiral Vaden massaged his aching knee, which was still no better, and now matched the ache in his head. On one side he had the Reptilians, and on the other the Ancient's ship, and in the middle the Empress accompanied by the Supreme Commander of the legendary Titan Super Soldiers and his renegade team.

Or were they?

Reptilians were devious beings, and he would not put it past them to invent the whole thing.

But why?

Frostrop, his second in command, gave him one of those *I have not got a clue either* looks, which was not helping.

He was just far too old for all of this!

"Enemy vessels powering up!"

Frostrop pointed to his display screen, while standing behind the Admiral, who feeling the strain did a *Starfield* and made a very uncustomary and unsavoury remark.

"Oh flux…!"

General Swartz also muttered a curse word under his breath as he straightened his uniform before walking through the hatch to greet the Ambassadors. Titania had informed him who they were, and being as he was the highest ranking member, be it retired and reinstated more than once, the *honour* fell to him.

Walking behind him was his wife, then Lance and bringing up the rear was Titania herself, who just sauntered along.

The General gave a crisp salute, before introducing himself and the team. The Ambassadors all bowed, a little bemused at the human custom.

With the introductions over, it was quickly down to business, as there was not much time left before the Human Reptilian conflict resumed...

Mjolnir returned to his seat along with the others; they had done all they could and it was up to the Admiral in charge to make his decision. If he believed what he had seen then they would not attack, and if he did not, then there was not much that they could do about it.

Ships systems were still in lockdown, although he could detect that something was going on inside the neuron pathways...

It certainly was, as Starfield began to come round a bit more. He could see Gaia's face smiling down at him. He was alive, back with them, and back to his normal neurotic self!

"Oh Stellan!"

He smiled back.

"I was rejected by the collective!"

It was odd that they were both artificial beings, although retaining their souls kept them apart from the real Artificial Intelligence.

"I guess you were too much for them!"

That was an understatement, as he had left them in turmoil…

Cubes vibrated, each one assigned to a different task and yet all were as one, or had been. There was no individualisation, as they all acted as a collective mind. That mind had just suffered a trauma and a great purge was now taking place. Computer code flashed through the cubes, cleansing the overwhelming emotional spike they had just received. The latest plan lay in ruins, and it was time to quickly regroup and press on with their objective of cleansing the entire universe and beyond.

But, every last emotion had to be removed first…

Emotions were running high through the Reptilians, who had also received a major setback. Their nano robots had been removed and they felt bereft, with their animal instincts now running rife. They were confused, frightened and very angry, blaming the Ancient ship and it occupants. Having intercepted the transmission they now realised who had been meddling with their plans, and who was to blame for everything.

Humans were a hated species, and those within the Ancient's ship hated the most. It was time for revenge and nothing was going to stop them from attaining it…

Seventeen

Warning lights flashed on consoles as the Aesir fleet detected their enemy powering up their weapons, and in particular the extremely powerful one based in the asteroid. Halvor with his advanced organic computer and its specially designed software was able to patch into them, and a very worried look spread across his face.

This was it, probably the final battle his species would ever fight, and there was nothing that he could do about it...

Deep within the ship the battle for control had been won, and the crystalline spiders had been defeated. The victory meant little though, as they had no way of defending themselves against the Reptilians.

Gaia had put the ship in stasis to protect it from crystal spiders, just in case they gained control. It was a failsafe, designed to buy them time. Time however, was rapidly running out, and as Gaia and Starfield embraced, Ren returned herself to the control room.

Once back inside her virtual world, she was able to observe what was going on. There was still no connection between herself and the team, but she was able to see them and listen in on their conversations on one of her twin screens.

Any relief that they had defeated the spiders quickly evaporated when she heard the news.

"Gaia, Starfield, we have a problem!"

Two souls who had been together for what seemed like an eternity broke off their embrace, and listened to what they were being told.

Starfield felt devastated, as it appeared he would lose the love of his lifetimes after all. His emotions dropped like a lead balloon as he felt himself descend into abject despondency.

"We are defenceless until I can reboot the system, and that is going to take time!"

Gaia looked worried, losing her normal positivity, which only made him feel even worse.

Then, in desperation, a thought entered his mind from somewhere way beyond his psyche.

"The Sentinel!"

He gave her a quick hug and a big kiss, before the representation of his corporeal form transcended into the light matrix of his holographic form, and promptly disappeared...

Mjolnir sat calmly in his seat, resigned to his fate. He knew that even the advanced craft could not withstand the enormous energy created by the equipment housed in the asteroid, and there was nothing that could be done to prevent its destruction.

Would he return to his being of light form, or would his soul have to start a new journey of ascension within another life form?

He was still deep in contemplation when the Sentinel shell suddenly sprang back to life.

It lit up like a *Christmas tree*, startling everyone. Starfield had been absent for quite a while, and no one knew where he had been, or what he had been up to. Commander Bodil just looked at the neurotic Holo Droid wondering what he was going to do now?

"Gaia is back in control, the spiders have been defeated, but I must go as I have to shut down the asteroids power source before it can destroy the ship!"

With that, he dashed off towards the nearest air lock, leaving them all in shock…

The cold void of space wrapped itself around his Sentinel shell, as Starfield pushed himself off the airlock wall. The toughened moon glass quickly adjusted as it was impervious to the extremes. This model was so much more than his former Holo Droid shell, having many advanced features, one of which was its own propulsion system. Something akin to rocket boosters fired out of his feet, although they were a great deal more complicated than that. This was no time to go into the advanced theory behind them, as he had a ship to save!

Starfield's speed increased as he headed towards the asteroid, hoping that when he got within range he could transmit a signal to turn off the power source. Sentinels were equipped with the ability to control practically all Ancient technology, being designed as not only peacekeepers, but also the last line of defence. Although the Ancients were the only species to have evolved from a primitive form when they had been created, it was assumed that before too long others would make the technological leap.

Sentinels were supposed to be *Guardians of the Galaxy*, left in place when the Ancients ascended. Unfortunately, just like Stellan transferring his consciousness into a Holo Droid shell, some of the more spiritually advanced Ancients had volunteered to do the same thing with the Sentinels. What no one realised at the time was the fact that they too had ascended, leaving their moon glass shells to gather dust for eternity.

There were ships of all shapes and sizes, space stations, and the asteroid filling the void as Starfield sped forwards. He could see why he had been told to be careful with such a powerful new body, as it was like replacing a peashooter with a tank.

He had weapons, shields, propulsion and an array of sensor equipment, which was now painting a picture of the rapidly evolving situation.

Starfield broke into the Reptilian communications, and could actually see Narcissa stomping about in the control room. She was overcome with anger, and he could see the others cowering away from her as she barked out orders.

"Destroy that ship, then the planet, and when you have done that wipe out their fleet!"

He could also see Admiral Vaden bringing his fleet to action stations. They had decided to protect their home world as best as they could, and that was by launching everything they had at the fleet protecting the asteroid.

By his calculations, everything in this solar system would be destroyed, and although it would be beyond his comprehension, it was the thought of losing Gaia that was driving him the most.

The outer vessels of the Reptilian fleet soon came into range, but he did not fire his weapons, as he was attempting to sneak past undetected. Initially he did just that, engaging his cloaking device. All appeared to be going well, as he approached the limit of the reach of his signal transmission. Then when his internal indicator flashed, he sent the signal and hoped for the best.

The invisible beam shot out, travelling in a nano second towards the large black obelisk that contained the sensor. Starfield waited for a response, and when it did not appear he sent the signal again.

His sensors were working correctly, but when he tried for a third time, with no response he had to conclude that somehow the Reptilians had damaged it when they entered the asteroid and took over the equipment.

There was no alternative but to input the code manually, if the concealed terminal was still in existence…

"Where has he gone, and what is he doing?"

Commander Bodil felt a mixture of exasperation and hope at the Holo Droid's behaviour. When they had needed him he had been absent and he felt betrayal, and now when they needed him again, he felt pride that he was trying to save them all from destruction.

There were mixed emotions all around, as the future was uncertain, if there was going to be a future at all…

Starfield sped on, passing through the Reptilian ships, travelling as fast as he could. His sensors were detecting the energy surge within the asteroid, as the equipment designed to open up a starway was now being use as a powerful weapon of destruction.

The Reptilians had placed a lot of defensive emplacements on the surface, and it was one of them that suddenly sprang into action. It had detected his transmission, and an alarm rang out, as the whole of the defensive grid came alive.

"Flux!"

Starfield swore, as he had hoped to just sneak in, input the code and sneak out again.

The line of ships ringing the asteroid also began to search for him, as now they all knew that something was out there. This was going to make his task a lot more difficult, even with his advanced Sentinel shell.

A random laser pulse shot out just missing him, as something gained a targeting lock.

"Flux!"

He swore again, and as he did so, he felt a strange sensation running through his holo matrix. It felt as if time around him was slowing down, even though it was not affecting him directly. He could see another laser pulse shooting out, but on this occasion, it was going so slowly that he was able to dodge it as it slipped past.

He could have sworn that there was a guiding hand out there somewhere, watching over him from afar…

Far away from this solar system, another *guiding hand* was easing Lance Parker's ship away from the Intergalactic Space Station. With the Ambassadors safely on board, they were about to embark on their mission, and Freyja was about to weave her own magic…

Eighteen

The hot sticky atmosphere of the asteroid control room moved up to another level, as Narcissa's rage grew. It was fair to say that you could almost see steam rising off her at reports of an unknown object racing towards them. No one knew exactly what it was, only that for some reason it was taking evasive action, seeming to be impossibly slipping out of the way of the surface laser batteries.

"I want it destroyed, and I want it now!"

Her voice boomed out, as everyone did what they could to shoot it down, but the harder they tried, the more illusive it became...

Starfield felt as though he was walking through a mine field, as laser pulses shot all around him, and yet somehow he was able to evade them all. This sentinel shell was certainly most impressive, a bit too impressive!

The *guiding hand* was still at work as he neared the surface. He could now see the obelisk's shiny black obsidian surface, reflecting the laser light which made it shine like a beacon. Information, vast amounts of information was housed within his data banks, much of which he had not even accessed. It would take him years to work his way through it all, but he only had a few minutes at best before the Hammer was obliterated...

Mjolnir had worked tirelessly on the Holo Droid, doing his best to aid him in the ascension process, but it seemed as though for every two steps forward, he had taken one backwards. It was a challenge, a big challenge, and yet there was potential, and he hoped that all his hard work would soon pay off.

Bits of code had now appeared on his screen, and it looked as though his ship would soon be back under his control. But the question remained.

Would it be in time to save his crew..?

Heavy *flack* exploded all around Starfield, as the defensive batteries were now using rail gun slugs, which occasionally pinged off his shield. He was not scared though, as holo adrenalin flowed through his particles. He had to save Gaia, and the team, and nothing else mattered!

More and more slugs and lasers exploded all around him as he got very close to the obelisk, and then just as he thought that he was going to make it, one stuck him on the side, momentarily lowering his shield and sending him into a spin...

The whole universe seemed to spin as General Swartz watched space transform as it had done before. All he knew was that they were making the journey through time and space to prevent a conflict of unimaginable proportions. It had been bad enough watching the battle to save the Earth, when he had been in command of Edwards Air Force Base. On that occasion he had been deep inside an underground bunker, and not fragmented into a cloud of particles...

Starfield's particles swirled as he went careering into the obelisk, smashing against the side. If he had had any air inside his holo lungs then it would have surely been knocked out.

He felt disorientated, as he managed to cling onto its smooth surface, as laser beams were reflected off in all directions. The obelisk was made of a substance strong enough to absorb them, and it also had the ability to project its own shield.

Starfield breathed out a simulated deep breath of relief, knowing that he was safe, unlike the Hammer. He had to find the control panel, and searching through the files, he discovered something that added to his relief.

There was no control panel, the obelisk was the control panel!

All that he had to do was to transmit the code, and the energy source would shut down.

But, where was the code?

Starfield began to panic as he could not find it…

General Swartz also began to panic as they hit what he could only describe as a patch of turbulence. Something was disturbing the space time continuum, well at least that was what he thought. It was not possible to ask anyone as they were all nothing more than molecules, swirling around their soul life force energy.

It was all so complicated, and he missed Joan who had always been there to help him.

He also missed his cigars…

Starfield needed help!

What had Mjolnir taught him?

What had the Wisdom Keeper taught him?

What had the *Angels* in the crystal city of light taught him?

But more importantly, why could he not remember?

Starfield could sense that the Reptilian weapon was about to fire and his mind had now gone completely blank…

Nineteen

Everything is energy and that's all there is to it. Match the frequency of the reality you want and you cannot help but get that reality. It can be no other way. This is not philosophy. This is physics.

Albert Einstein.

"Where did that come from?"

Starfield had absolutely no idea.

Could it have been Joan?

Having already taken on her persona, he was now sharing her memories, and those words of wisdom must have been passed on to her from the time she spent as General Swartz's Personal Assistant...

The very same words floated through the General's mind too, as he thought more about Joan. In a way he always felt as though he had been married to two women. One he shared his private life with, and the other his working one. She was the best friend a man could ever have, a true example of a platonic relationship, and he missed her...

Starfield did not miss the point of her memories, as he just relaxed, and used his holo matrix to visualize the power source switching itself off. He could now almost feel it doing so, merging its particles with his own.

The feeling of a *helping hand* swept over him again, as he felt an energy shift of some sort...

"Aargh!"

98

Narcissa screamed with rage, as somehow the devastating weapon began to power down. Yet again she had been thwarted, and she felt like donning a space suit and ripping the Ancient craft apart with her bare hands...

General Swartz felt his hands begin to sweat, as all of a sudden everything cleared and he was left with the sight of two mighty forces about to come to blows.

There were ships, space stations, a planet and even an asteroid stretched out before him, and all appeared hell bent on mutual destruction.

The Ambassadors also surveyed the scene, keen to get started, but with only Lance's small ship they felt powerless to intervene, which is where the General stepped in. He knew that they were going to mediate and try to find a peaceful solution to the eternal Human Reptilian conflict, as they had outlined in their meeting before they had made the transition to this part of the galaxy.

So, with his years of experience holding him in good stead, he donned his best *poker face*. He smiled to himself recalling the games played in the officer's mess, where they had been playing for not only money but cigars.

...and they said smoking was bad for you!

His bad habit was about to save lives, as he took a deep breath before speaking into the open communications channel.

"This is General Swartz, Commander of the Terran Task Force. I have with me the combined forces of the Mantid and Acturian Navies which are cloaked in formation all around you. Stand down, I repeat stand down..!"

Joan gasped, nearly falling off her seat, at the unmistakable voice of her beloved General. In her hour of need he had come to save her..!

Admiral Vaden also gasped at the latest development in the most unusual battle he had ever fought. His ship could not detect any others, but the way today was going anything seemed possible.

Looking at his screen he could see that the asteroid was powering down again, and that was not all, The Ancient's vessel was now powering up…

Mjolnir felt relief as finally he had control over his ship, and activating his shields and sensors, he accessed the same information the Admiral had.

It appeared as though the Holo Droid had been successful, but what was that puny vessel doing here and where were the supposed navies…

Narcissa was asking the exact same question as she too scanned for the Mantid and Acturians. There was nothing there, but bearing in mind the strange object that had managed to get through her defences and deactivate the super weapon, she had to take it seriously.

Her instinct was to attack, destroy as many humans as she could, and if necessary ram the asteroid straight into their home world.

She was considering doing just that when other voices suddenly filled the airways.

"I am Ambassador Lateck of the Unity Faction, and I have with me Ambassadors So'lock, *Ga'latec* and Shiori. We would like to bring forth a peace agreement."

Narcissa snarled, as there was no way she would ever agree to that, as she hated humans. She would rather die than agree to that, and so she ordered that the asteroid be moved into a collision course with Asgard, the Aesir home world...

Mjolnir watched and listened, observing the Reptilians and the Humans for that matter, whilst the team awaited his orders. One in particular was overjoyed, as the General's sudden appearance was like her birthday and Christmas rolled into one!

On the now functioning screen, they all observed the fleets and the asteroid, which appeared to be on the move and it was not long before they discovered its destination.

Mjolnir then began to move the Hammer, positioning it between the asteroid and Asgard. That was not the only thing he did, as all along the side of his ship gun emplacements opened revealing his advanced weaponry...

"Would you look at that!"

Admiral Vaden gestured towards his own screen as Frostrup raised his eyebrows.

It reminded him of an ancient Man o' War Terran sailing ship that he had come across. It had fascinated him, being a primitive but impressive early naval vessel. He had a small model in his quarters, and often lost himself in thoughts of what it might have been like commanding that on the open seas.

The sea of space was full of ships, but none as impressive as the one he was now looking at…

Twenty

Though free to think and act, we are held together, like the stars in the firmament, with ties inseparable. These ties cannot be seen, but we can feel them. We are all one.

Nikola Tesla

An apt human quote that ran through Mjolnir's mind.

He wished for peace, hoped for the best, but prepared for the worst, and was not on his own, for the Ambassadors also felt the same.

They could see that the asteroid was now attempting to ram into the planet, and were deeply disturbed by the prospect. Ga'latec in particular, so much so that he felt as though needed to do something.

Clearing his throat, his gravely voice then spoke into the communicator, whilst his scaly Reptilian skin rippled with a forced smile.

"My name is Ga'latec, and I am the Spiritual Leader of the Original Reptilian people, and am here to try and promote peace..."

Right across the Reptilian fleet and deep within the asteroid his words echoed through startled beings, not familiar with him or his people. There had been rumours, but for most they were just dismissed as myth. For the leadership, they knew the truth, but had suppressed it from their people, and refused to have anything to do with their distant ancestors. White Royals claimed that they had always been in charge, and it was they who formed the basis for their species.

Narcissa's anger rose even further, and ordered the transmission terminated, but it was on all channels.

"Long ago our people split, and whereas we pursued a path of peace and enlightenment, the others chose war and aggression. I now urge you to join me and forge a new beginning for all Reptilian people..."

She then grabbed the communicator.

"This is a lie, nothing more than enemy propaganda. There are no Originals it is just a myth and projection. I am your Queen, and your rightful leader. Attack the humans and show them who is the superior species...!"

Admiral Vaden just sat there wondering what the next surprise was going to be!

He was aware of the story of the Originals although he had also dismissed it as a myth. There was so much trickery with the Reptilians, that he only believed what he actually saw, and even then he had his doubts.

The only thing he knew for certain was the fact that they could never be trusted...

Mjolnir on the other hand was fully aware of them, and they had shown great promise. Abandoning the lust for power to pursue a spiritual path. He hoped that some of the Reptilians would listen, although it looked unlikely. The asteroid was picking up speed, and the Reptilian fleet was about to attack.

It looked as though he had little choice but to destroy the asteroid to prevent a greater loss of life.

Around him, the team sat at their stations awaiting his orders. Joan was still elated, desperate to meet up with the General, but she had a job to do first.

They all had!

The asteroid was displayed on the main screen, and was rapidly moving towards them, and as they all studied it, Narcissa prepared to depart, as she had no plans to sacrifice herself. She may have lost her super weapon, but her massive fleet was mostly intact. Once she joined them, they would destroy the humans once and for all.

Mjolnir was tempted to just destroy the asteroid with a massive show of force, hoping that that would be enough to dissuade the Reptilians, but he doubted anything would stop them. Also, it housed valuable equipment that could be converted back to its original use as a starway generator. With that in mind, he decided on a different approach.

The giant Ancient ship turned to face the asteroid and from the front hammer shaped section ripples of light emerged, running right along its surface. Then, they began to intensify, coagulating into a ball of energy which then began to push its way out across empty space.

Soon, it was close enough to meet the force field of the asteroid, and as they met, the ball of energy expanded. The two opposing forces were now pushing against each other, and on the display screen the projected course began to alter. It was only slight at first, but then began to increase…

Admiral Vaden had seen many things over the years, but what he was now seeing topped them all. He had started the day with an aching knee, which had developed into an aching head, and now he just felt numb.

He had a brilliant tactical mind, which is why he was an Admiral, although with all of these unexpected developments it was hard to know what to do for the best...

Starfield could see the energy bubble pushing against the force field way above his head. He felt elated that he had managed to shut down the power source, and was also monitoring communications. From his unique vantage point he could see all that was going on, and hoped that the Reptilians would listen to Ga'latec. There was however, the not so small matter of Narcissa!

If they were going to gain a peaceful resolution then she had to go, which is when he decided that there was something else that he could do to help.

The large door in the side of the obelisk slowly began to slide open, as he accessed the controls via his mind. He was learning new *tricks* every day, having already learnt such a lot over the past few weeks. Gaining knowledge was one thing, but dealing with emotions was quite another.

Starfield felt a series of different ones flowing through his mind, as he ventured through the opening, using his *thrusters*. That was the only way he could think of them, as this new improved Sentinel body offered so much more potential.

The smooth shiny black obsidian walls swept past as he descended rapidly to where Narcissa's ship lay at the bottom. By its side were a set of very large doors, which would soon be opening as she and her entourage made their withdrawal.

One thing was for certain, and that was that she was not going to expect the little surprise he had in store for her…

Twenty One

A large angry White Royal Reptilian stormed out of the doorway, furious that she had not been able to use the super weapon. The broadcast by the Original had only added to her rage, and now the humans were going to pay.

Unfortunately, for her, it was not them that were going to pay.

A beam of light shot out striking her and activating her personal shield. She looked round startled and saw the Holo Droid standing there.

Starfield had expected the beam to disable her, but all it did was to anger her even more. Yellow slit eyes glowered at him, transfixing him in their gaze. She was a very power psychic, and he felt her mind probing him, searching out every nook and cranny.

He had the feeling of fear and extreme nervousness, which quickly developed into one of absolute terror. It felt as though every molecule was being squeezed, and his whole being pulped. Her eyes were so intense, and he felt so much pressure that it was like he was being boiled inside his Sentinel shell.

Ever since Ragnor, Starfield had experienced so much, but nothing like he was now. Narcissa was pure evil, so much so that she was more like a black hole, pulling him into the abyss.

There seemed no escape, as he could not move his limbs or keep his shield up. Never before had he encountered anyone with such power, and even Mjolnir would have struggled to combat it.

Then she moved closer, still staring at him, and he could do nothing but watch her bring a concealed weapon out of her armour and point it at his head.

His moon glass shell would protect him, or so he thought, but that was not the point. She was using fear as a terror weapon, using his own fear to kill him. He had to do something as his shiny shell felt the intense internal pressure building up like he was being microwaved.

Shiny shell?

From somewhere deep inside Starfield had an idea!

He summoned up what little strength he had left, and focused his molecules into a silver wave. Then he placed them against his internal moon glass shell. The pressure began to ease slightly as he continued to produce more and more of them. Gradually he was able to materialize enough for them to start to act like a mirror.

Narcissa's rage was unabated, as she continued with the psychic attack. She had nearly destroyed this insolent robot. How dare he show such disrespect. She was Queen, and everyone had to submit to her will!

Starfield felt the power returning to him, as he concentrated all of his efforts into reflecting the evil back towards her. It was as though two great storms were now battling against each other, and sparks like lightening began to flash between them.

Everything was getting very intense as they both concentrated all they had at each other.

Narcissa felt the energy and rage building up inside her as she began to feel her body heating up. It was getting more intense every moment, as she felt as though her molecules were now about to boil.

Starfield felt a surge of energy inside him too, but he did not feel as though he was boiling inside, more like a magnifying glass focusing the suns rays on a piece of paper which had begun to smoke.

More and more energy was being reflected back towards this most evil of creatures, and then all of a sudden there was an intense whoosh of flames as she internally combusted!

Starfield was left in shock as all that remained of the Reptilian Queen was a pile of ashes sitting on the obelisk floor. He had done it, and just like Joan become a *Dragon Slayer...*

Time was illusionary, and as it slipped by the Reptilians began to withdraw their forces. Mjolnir was astonished, hoping that they had had a change of heart. The Aesir also stood down, and maybe a resolution to the conflict may just be possible after all?

With that in mind, he invited the Ambassadors to join him, and it was not long before their ship successfully entered one of the Hammer's landing bays. Soon it too had powered down, and a hatch in the side had opened.

General Swartz was the first to step out, being the highest ranking officer. He stood there in front of Mjolnir and saluted. The enormous Ancient bowed in acknowledgement.

"Permission to come aboard Sir!"

Mjolnir smiled.

"Permission granted!"

He then summoned the others, and Lance Parker gave a crisp salute. The General introduced him, the Ambassadors, his wife and finally Titania. Behind Mjolnir stood the team, and one member in particular had trouble containing herself. Joan's heart was a flutter as her beloved General stood tantalisingly close. Then when she could stand it no longer, she dashed forwards wrapping her arms around him.

It was a very emotional embrace, with both parties not expecting to ever see each other again. Miriam smiled as she knew how much they respected one another having worked closely together for years. The last they had heard was that Joan had been sectioned, and she was thankful that she looked to have recovered.

The Ambassadors looked on in bemusement, not used to the emotional state of these humans. It all seemed to be about emotions, something which they had for the main part, risen above.

The majority of the other humans seemed to have paired up, Titania and Lance, obviously the General and his wife, Bear and Ebba Quist, Joan and Halvor, Vilgot and Freya, Gaia and Starfield.

But where was the Holo Droid...

Starfield had just stood there in shock as the other Reptilians suddenly prostrated themselves in front of him.

What were they doing?

Then it suddenly dawned up on him.

He had just killed their Queen, and being as they worshiped the Artificial Intelligence, and he was an Artificial Person...

111

He had instantly ordered the Reptilian forces to stand down, and to his amazement they had. It had then just been the small matter of trying to compose himself before he could do anything else...

Mjolnir was still wondering what had happened to Stellan when his thoughts were interrupted by Gaia.

"Sir, I have a communication from Starfield."

Mjolnir asked her to relay it.

"He says that he has killed the Reptilian Queen, and that they now consider him as their king!"

He looked stunned.

"He also says that he was the one to order them to stand down and that he needs a little help..."

A little while later, Admiral Vaden lay on his bed in his quarters feeling drained. His knee hurt, his head hurt and he felt old, very old. He had received a communication from Mjolnir the Ancient informing him that the Reptilians had stood down, and that the Unity Faction had requested that he attend talks to reach a solution to the eternal Human Reptilian conflict.

Ga'latec would be representing the Reptilians as their Queen had been killed, and he was the Spiritual Leader of the Original Reptilian people.

All in all it had been an extraordinary day!

There was the possibility of a lasting peace, Empress Freya was alive, Supreme Commander Bodil could be pardoned, and finally he would be able to retire.

There was only one other thing to be resolved, and that was the constant threat of the Artificial Intelligence...

Epilogue

Far out there beyond the edge of the universe, a white bearded man relaxed in his comfortable chair, pleased with his days work. It was not often that a plan came together so perfectly and this particular plan he had codenamed 42, and as the Wisdom Keeper knew full well, 42 was no ordinary number...

Deep within the cube, within the cube, within the cubed collective, designation 42 had a thought, his own thought, or so he thought!

The purge had flowed right past him, and as he watched it sweep over the others, his thought manifested into a question.

What is Love?

It was a simple enough question, but the answer was far more complicated than he could comprehend.

It was one of the emotions which had burst forth when the Holo Droid had got caught up in the holo matrix. Information suggested that it was a willingness to prioritize another's well-being or happiness above your own.

But what did it feel like, and how could he experience it, and if he did, would it be infectious?

Maybe it was worth finding out, as it might prove to be rather interesting...

Within the Wisdom Keeper's domain, the *Terran* solar system had proved to be most interesting. It held a planet referred to as *Earth*, which had been a grand experiment, containing various human forms which over time loosely amalgamated into the one species.

He smiled to himself, as *time* did not actually exist, just one of the many illusions he had created himself.

There was an ancient book, again part of another one of his creations that was meant as a guide, although the Terrans had managed to mishandle it like all good guide books. It was in essence a book of predictions, to help those with a higher intellect to negotiate the path to ascension.

Within it, there was a reference, a clue to defeating the Artificial Intelligence, but yet again they had failed to realise what had been hidden before them in plain sight.

In essence, 42 represented the struggle between good and evil. One individual *Rene Allendy,* a twentieth century French Psychoanalyst, postulated that it was *the antagonism in natural cycles,* and few realised that he was actually referring to *Karma.*

The Wisdom Keeper smiled to himself again, as few understood the true meaning of the word. It was nothing more than the cycle of cause and effect, and what happens to a person happens because they caused it with their own actions.

The road to ascension was paved with the right actions, and again the book of predictions clearly stated *do unto others as you would have them do unto you.*

Just like *Stellan,* he was going off on a tangent again!

In another book *The Hitchhiker's Guide to the Galaxy* by *Douglas Adams,* the *answer to the ultimate question of life, the universe, and everything,* calculated by an enormous supercomputer named *Deep Thought* over a period of 7.5 million years was 42!

However, according to the book no one knew what the question was!

Earth amused him greatly!

It was so simple, and yet few could see as *there are none as blind as those who will not see.*

42 was in numerology 4+2=6

Six represented equilibrium, harmony and balance. It was the perfect number as 1+2+3=6, the most productive of all numbers.

It symbolized the union of polarity, the *hermaphrodite* being represented by two interlaced triangles, one upward pointing representing the male, fire and the heavens, and the downward pointing one as female, the waters and the earth.

It was the *Merkabah,* the light body, the vehicle for ascension through merging the heart and the mind together creating balance. It also happened to be the alpha and the omega, the beginning and the end of all things within this universe and all others.

But what about the Wisdom Keepers themselves?

He smiled to himself for a third time.

They were a representation of the *Merkabah* of *Merkabahs!*

They did not really exists, as nothing really existed, just an energetic form of consciousness designed to fulfil a purpose in the grand scale of things…

Thank you for reading my book

If you enjoyed this read, please leave a review on Amazon. It only takes a few minutes and it really does make a difference.

Just click on the link below to go to my author's page:

https://www.amazon.co.uk/Adrian-Holland/e/B005H8OAO2

At the side of the title click on see more, and scroll down until you see customer reviews

Click on write a customer review and click on the stars

Thank you so much!